SUITE ENCOUNTERS

SUITE ENCOUNTERS
HOTEL SEX STORIES

Edited by
Rachel Kramer Bussel

Copyright © 2012 by Rachel Kramer Bussel.

All rights reserved. Except for brief passages quoted in newspaper, magazine, radio, television, or online reviews, no part of this book may be reproduced in any form or by any means, electronic or mechanical, including photocopying or recording, or by information storage or retrieval system, without permission in writing from the publisher.

Published in the United States by Cleis Press, Inc.,
2246 Sixth Street, Berkeley, California 94710.

Printed in the United States.
Cover design: Scott Idleman/Blink
Cover photograph: Image Source
Text design: Frank Wiedemann

First Edition.
10 9 8 7 6 5 4 3 2 1

Trade paper ISBN: 978-1-57344-790-4
E-book ISBN: 978-1-57344-802-4

Contents

vii   *Introduction: Sex Magic*

1   *Two-Way* • ARIEL GRAHAM
9   *Selfish* • DONNA GEORGE STOREY
23   *Air-Conditioning. Color TV. Live Mermaids* • ANNA MEADOWS
32   *Proof of Desire* • REMITTANCE GIRL
39   *Soundproof* • EMILY MORETON
47   *An Inspector Comes* • SUZANNE FOX
60   *Surrender with a Twist* • SULEIKHA SNYDER
73   *Unbound at the Holiday Inn* • LILY K. CHO
83   *Travelodge Tess* • JUSTINE ELYOT
95   *Business Expenses* • ELIZABETH SILVER
107   *Return to the Nonchalant Inn* • EROBINTICA
115   *The Deacon* • TAHIRA IQBAL
127   *Love, Loud as a Bomb* • STEVE ISAAK
133   *Night School* • VALERIE ALEXANDER
145   *Feel So Dirty* • ANDREA DALE
155   *Please Come Again* • TENILLE BROWN
163   *Dirty White Envelope* • ELLIE VOKES
169   *Tailgating at the Cedar Inn* • DELILAH DEVLIN
182   *Stiletto's Big Score* • MICHAEL A. GONZALES
192   *Special Request* • RACHEL KRAMER BUSSEL

205   *About the Authors*
209   *About the Editor*

INTRODUCTION: SEX MAGIC

Hotel rooms are magical. Anything can happen in them, and the travelers in these stories know that well, using their hotel and motel rooms to engage in all sorts of explosive acts.

Sex work is, of course, a mainstay of hotel sex, but in this anthology, sex work happens with a twist. There's the male escort and a desk clerk in "Night School," by Valerie Alexander, the "Dirty White Envelope" in Ellie Vokes's story and the professional procurer in my "Special Request." Hotel workers play just as vibrant a role here as traditional sex workers.

Hotels give us an opportunity to engage in our favorite forms of sex magic on big, wide beds with plenty of pillows that can be used to lean back on or muffle screams of pleasure. We can indulge in the guilty pleasure of eavesdropping on our neighbors or walking down the hall hoping to spy or hear something juicy. Many of the characters here use hotels to escape from their everyday lives and engage in all sorts of flings and fetishes. Hotels bring out our most daring side, and let us strip down in a window, listen in on a stranger, star in an orgy and take part in all manner of other outrageous sex acts.

In "Two-Way," by Ariel Graham, a couple rekindles their passion for hotel sex and exhibitionism, recalling past thrills while making new ones. Isabel, in Donna George Storey's "Selfish," sets out at age forty-four to try something new and a little risky, and her daring and selfishness pay off big time. The title of Anna Meadows's "Air-Conditioning. Color TV. Live Mermaids" tells you a good bit of what her story's about, but there's a tenderness and longing in this beautiful tale of a real mermaid and the man who wants—and gets—her that you'll have to read to fully appreciate.

The characters in Remittance Girl's "Proof of Desire" get exactly that, and in her telling, it's hot, urgent and fierce: "There it was. Need, desire so strong it burst into the stillness of the room, tainting the air with an ache. It hurt. It hurt deliciously to stand so close, to see the beads of sweat that birthed and glinted along the line of his sternum. To smell the faded scent of morning soap rise off his skin, and the sweetness of the oil he'd used on his cock, and the richer musk of his crotch. The tip of her tongue prickled with want."

The hotel in "Soundproof," by Emily Moreton, is anything but, and listening to strangers get it on fuels Sam's desire as he soaks in every word. Suzanne Fox teases us with a fun yet sexy murder mystery weekend in "An Inspector Comes"—yes, her use of the double entendre is deliberate. "Surrender with a Twist," by Suleikha Snyder, takes us to, fittingly, Las Vegas; no book of hotel erotica would be complete without some Sin City sex. Lily K. Cho brings on the kink in "Unbound at the Holiday Inn," as a marriage takes a vital step when Mark bares his bottom for a spanking, changing the course of their relationship for the better. "Travelodge Tess" is on the job, but that doesn't stop her from having some fun along the way in Justine

Elyot's clever tale. Elizabeth Silver delivers a torrid threesome in "Business Expenses," as Margo, Tonya and Javier enjoy sex toys—and each other.

The tone becomes nostalgic in Erobintica's "Return to the Nonchalant Inn," when Gerald and Jillian return to the island hotel they'd visited twenty years before and figure out if they can pick up where they left off. Tahira Iqbal looks at the head of a hotel empire, a modern-day Conrad Hilton named Mark Deacon, in "The Deacon," as this corporate tycoon makes sure to do a very thorough inspection of his hotels, and a very special employee. Steve Isaak's brief but powerful "Love, Loud as a Bomb" deals with the fear induced by a Hawaiian tsunami, and a clairvoyant who times her orgasm to a disaster.

Stories about sex workers abound in erotica, but they are usually women; "Night School" mixes things up with its male escort and a woman who turns him on to the thrill of being dominated. They exchange power in a way that unsettles and energizes them both: "He looked at the wall with this weird smile and I realized just how embarrassed he really was. I was the one whose presence had been requested tonight and he was the one who had done the requesting. He didn't know who was the client here, him or me, and the ambiguity had robbed him of his usual confidence."

In "Feel So Dirty," by Andrea Dale, a storm knocks out the power, but that doesn't stop Lea and Jon from skirting the edges of an affair as they enjoy a sexual connection that the close proximity of their hotel rooms enhances. "Please Come Again," by Tenille Brown, manages to tackle homelessness in a way that doesn't address it as an "issue" but rather looks at the core of humanity and desire for human touch Randall hasn't lost, and that Simone welcomes as she takes care of him, sexually and otherwise.

Role-playing takes center stage in "Dirty White Envelope," which opens with, "It took me three years to tell Ron I wanted to be treated like a whore," and goes from there with this common, exciting fantasy. Erotic romance author Delilah Devlin gives us "Tailgating at the Cedar Inn," in which Kelsey brazenly takes on two guys who are more than happy to enjoy her lusty attention. Michael A. Gonzales gives us a sexy heroine, Miki Jamison, a forty-five-year-old former blaxploitation star who luxuriates in the sumptuous hotel room, and her costar's passion for her. Closing out the book, Francine is famous for being able to deliver anything to her guests by "Special Request," and when Claudine requests she arrange—and attend—an orgy, she is more than up to the challenge—or so she thinks.

All of these stories capture some aspect of the thrill of hotel sex, and I hope you will enjoy them at home, at a hotel or wherever you happen to be, and perhaps you'll be inspired on your next vacation, staycation, work trip, or wherever your travels take you, to engage in the spirit of these sexy stories.

Rachel Kramer Bussel
New York City

TWO-WAY

Ariel Graham

"Have we stayed here before?" Mia asked as Tom struggled to free their suitcase from the elevator. The luggage was blue and wheeled and on a leash and apparently the wheels had been taken from a recalcitrant grocery cart because the thing balked at the slightest imperfection on any surface, squalling like mad on the end of its tether.

Tom glanced at her as another passenger who wanted to go up more floors gave the bag a push to get it, and Tom, out of the elevator.

"Oh, yeah. I forgot about you and hotels." He grinned and his dark hair fell into his eyes. At thirty-five, after seven years of marriage, he still looked like the twenty-eight-year-old she'd seen pitching a softball for the software corporation they both worked for. That had begun her brief—very brief—flirtation with company softball, which had actually been a flirtation with Tom. The softball had ended the day he asked her out. No one on the team had begged her to change her mind.

She'd hated softball. She loved Tom. And chocolate, and traveling, and the autonomy of huge crowds at conventions where a name tag and registration fee allowed her to become anyone she wanted. So much public around her made her a little exhibitionistic.

Hotel rooms did, too. The privacy imparted by a key card held by so many guests before her made her feel she was onstage the entire time she was in a hotel room. She imagined narrators describing her every movement as she unpacked her bag or got dressed or undressed, talked on the phone or ate instant oatmeal. There was just something about the sheer number of people who had been there before her that made her feel watched—and she didn't mind it in the least.

They moved together through the boxy hallways strewn with vast desert landscapes that made no sense—they'd just flown from desert, from the software company's corporate headquarters in Phoenix to arrive at the anonymous hotel in L.A.

She caught Tom's eye, about to point out the questionable decor, but Tom beat her to it.

"I know, and I'm sure the Phoenix hotel has ocean prints."

She grinned at him and ran her hand through her sleek platinum hair that ended shaved on her nape. "Or more convoluted, maybe forest and desert and mountain and plains and all the others are mixed and matched like a giant multiple choice test and if you can just figure out which hotel's decor goes with which hotel's location—"

Tom stopped walking and used his taller, broader, bulkier body to press her into the wall. "If you will please, *please* stop talking about this, I promise I will fuck you silly when we get inside." He grinned down at her and Mia licked her lips and tucked her index fingers through his front belt loops.

"And yes, we stayed here two years ago for the unveiling

of Enterprise Fox. I introduced you to my fraternity brother, Derrick, who's assistant manager?"

She nodded, not convinced, and he grinned. "Well, anyway, you liked it." One of his front teeth had a slight chip and was the tiniest bit crooked. With his mouth closed, he was almost impossibly male-model handsome, and then he'd grin and be her Tom.

Teasing, she said, "Were the paintings this much of a test then?"

He glanced at her. "Remember our deal?"

"It does sound promising," she said, releasing him. "Let's hurry." And she went down the hallway without him, looking right and left for their room number, until he whistled and cocked his head in the correct direction, the opposite of hers. She loved hotels but she routinely got lost in them.

The layout of their room brought the hotel back for her better than the fact that they'd stayed there for the release of Enterprise Fox. While Tom went off with the ice bucket on a quest, Mia unpacked, staring at herself through the eyes of the invisible audience. Whenever they were out in public, she was aware of them, the muscled six feet of Tom, his dark skin and hair and eyes, and herself, all five feet of her with cropped cap of white-blonde hair and a bodybuilder's body.

She didn't mind being in front of people. She didn't mind being looked at.

She kind of liked it.

The room featured a closet cubbyhole to the left just inside the door and the entrance to the bathroom on the right, an acre or so of cold linoleum and scanty towels to step out of the shower onto. Hotel bathrooms did nothing for her.

Past the entrance and the closet, there was an interior, adjoining room door, the kind that still used a key in a deadbolt rather than a card, and past the door there was a desk built into the wall and an armchair with a footstool, glass doors that opened onto a sort of balcony, and back in the room were two double beds side by side across from the armchair and desk.

What jogged her memory was the squat, square mirror over the desk. Not great for showing the corporate traveler just how corporate the business drag looked, but it did seem a lot like a corporate hotel's subtle nod at anonymous and possibly raunchy hotel sex.

Mia grinned, pushed the intransigent suitcase out of the way and sat down on the end of the bed across from the desk. Her pixie self grinned back at her and she remembered being there with Tom, the way he'd piled pillows up under her head so she could look down and see the two of them, and then turned them sideways on the bed so they could both watch. That had been two years and a lot of changes ago. They were better now. A lot better. But she remembered that time with a flash of heat that seemed to start at the base of her neck and shoot downward to her clit.

She took a breath, watching her chest move, and ran her hands over her breasts, cupping them, imagining someone on the other side of the mirror, watching. One-way or two-way, she could never remember what it was called when people on one side had a mirror and people on the other had a window. What she did remember was one of the TV news hour-long investigative shows that covered an unscrupulous landlord who riddled the apartment's bedrooms and baths in one family's home with cameras behind the mirrors so he could tape the mother and daughters. For them, it had been trauma. For Mia, it was the stuff of fantasy.

Just when she was beginning to wonder where Tom had gone and whether her ability to get lost absolutely anywhere had rubbed off, he reappeared, coming through the door of their room with loot.

"I got you a diet soda," Tom said, reappearing, and then started laughing. "What are you doing *now*?"

She was pressed up against the mirror trying to see whether or not a coin pressed to the surface cast a double inside the mirror. Not that it would tell her much because she couldn't remember which meant mirror/mirror and which meant mirror/window.

She just grinned and flipped the quarter in the air. "Don't hotel rooms make you feel like someone somewhere is watching you?"

Tom put the sodas and ice bucket down on one of the bedside tables. "No," he said in his *you're crazy but I love you* cautious voice. "They make *you* feel that way. They just make me feel grubby." But he came forward and put his arms around her and when she tugged the bedspread off the bed and his jeans down his legs, he climbed out of them and sat down on the end of the bed. Mia stood in front of him, still dressed, grinning. She kissed him and then, slowly, kissed down the length of his chest and across his abs and down the trail of dark hair that led to his thick, hard cock. The head was heavily beaded with precome. She grinned up at him, teasing, and touched just the tip of her tongue to his erection. Tom growled, laughing, then cupped the back of her head and forced his cock into her mouth, bumping the back of her throat, thrusting as he muttered something that made her pause. She couldn't very well ask, and he repeated himself anyway.

"That's a nice view." And a few minutes later: "Take your clothes off. Get on the bed and do that. I want to watch."

The words zeroed in on Mia's cunt. She got wetter, took a breath, sucked extra hard for just a minute and then slid off him, pulling her shirt and bra over her head as Tom stacked all the pillows on the bed. Her jeans came off next, and her thong. She grinned wickedly as he lay back, canted slightly on the bed, and when she crawled between his legs and knelt with her ass up, taking him deep in her mouth, he moaned.

"That's gorgeous. God, I can see how wet you are from here. Play with yourself."

Kneeling, she moved one hand around his balls and sank her mouth over him again. Her other hand went down between her legs, moving over her shaved pussy, spreading her juices over her hot, swollen lips, circling her clit until Tom made an inarticulate sound of need, and Mia found her own cunt with two fingers, pressing in and out to the beat of her mouth going up and down on Tom's shaft. She came, once, her core sucking at her fingers, clit throbbing with rings of pleasure, and Tom felt her pause, laughed with pleasure, sucked in breath when she started again and said, "No, come up here." Pulling her onto his chest, kissing her while she straddled his leg with both of hers, horny as a college kid in the backseat of a car.

"Turn around," he whispered, biting her lip and releasing, and she swung her legs over his hips, impaled her hot, wet, aching cunt on his cock and stared at herself in the mirror. Her cheeks were flushed, her biceps pumped, her nipples hard and red with blood. She watched her lips spread open as Tom sank himself deep inside her, watched the shine of her juices on her clit, the insides of her thighs.

"Ride," Tom said and she started to pump her hips, watching as her breasts bounced on her chest and her muscles flexed, forcing her up and down. She could watch Tom's cock disappearing into her, could see everything, and so could anyone else who might be watching. Not a mirror but a window. She imagined a group of people watching, like producers or directors or cameramen, people recording them, no stage directions. Even though it was a job for them, they'd be getting so turned on. She pumped harder, and thought of cameras, of the video going out into the world. Her hands crisscrossed her body. She fingered her clit, pressed hard, saw her head start to tip back before she lost sight of herself and it was all sensation, Tom taking up the rhythm and fucking her hard.

"I can see everything from here," Tom said from behind her. "I love watching that."

She grinned and didn't protest when a few minutes later he withdrew, flipped her over onto her back and pressed into her, looping her legs up over his shoulders, kneeling and plunging into her as hard and far as he could.

She turned her head, saw her own ecstatic face as she and Tom both started to come. Then her eyes closed and her thoughts stopped completely and for a while there was just pleasure.

They fell asleep together, holding each other close, reflected in the mirror over the desk at the end of the bed.

When she woke, only minutes had passed. Her body glowed and both of them were putting off heat, reflecting it back and forth between them. Tom stirred when she did, leaned down and kissed her, then sat, grinning a bit like the cat who'd swallowed the canary when really Mia had done a lot more swallowing.

"What?" she asked, a trifle suspicious. She wasn't sure at that point she'd want the public angle, the audience, the approving masses. She thought by now they'd be urging her to go take a shower with her sticky self.

"Well," Tom said, getting up to pull on just his underwear. "I thought you might like to see the video."

Mia's mouth fell open at the same time that she frowned. "What?"

Tom, grinning, held up an actual key on a stick, not a magnetic card. Mia shook her head, not understanding.

Tom pointed along the wall with the mirror, just to the left of the desk where the adjoining room's door was located, an inside door that still opened with a key on a stick.

Mia looked from Tom to key to door to mirror, mouth opening farther, shock turning to delight and disbelief.

"I thought for sure you'd seen the ice machine we passed coming in here and wondered where the hell I'd gone." He grinned. "Cost a bit to get them to go along with this, but Derrick's still assistant manager."

She sprang at him, wrapped her arms around his neck and kissed him hard. "I'll bet it's an excellent video," he said at last, untangling himself from her and heading to the room next door.

"I'll bet it's cause for instant replay," Mia said, and sat waiting for Tom to come back into the hotel room where, for once, she was content thinking it was just the two of them watching.

SELFISH

Donna George Storey

There's a first time for everything.

Isabel adjusted the strap of her shoulder bag. It was heavier than usual, which was not surprising given all the extra "supplies" inside. Squaring her shoulders, she turned to Christine, who was on duty at the register.

"I have an appointment at the bank, then some errands. I should be back by three."

Christine's forehead creased into a frown.

"They're not planning foreclosure or anything," Isabel said lightly. It was such a shame to mar that perfect, twenty-four-year-old skin with unnecessary worry. "It's a routine matter. No big deal."

But, of course, it was a big deal. A big fucking deal.

Do one thing for yourself every day. Something selfish. Simply because you want it.

As Isabel pulled into the Hyatt's underground parking lot, she figured she wasn't the only woman on earth who heard her therapist's voice in her head at critical moments. Wasn't that the point of therapy—to replace negative self-talk with a positive, life-enhancing monologue?

So far she'd carried out Tracy's assignment for the week perfectly. She'd asked her husband to make dinner *and* clean up when she hosted the last reading at the bookstore. She'd enlisted her daughter to pick up the organic veggie box from the farmers' market on her way home from play practice—a big time saver. She'd bought herself a new coffee mug, just because the color made her happy.

Today's indulgence was far more ambitious, however: rent a hotel room, seduce a stiff and proper banker, sweeten the deal with a very naughty ensemble of lingerie. She wasn't so sure her therapist would approve of that.

Isabel pulled up to the valet stand and shut off the engine. Her pulse was racing. And she hadn't even gotten to the hard part yet.

But there was a first time for everything. Even when you were forty-four.

Although at the moment, handing her keys to the chipper teenager in the valet's shirt, she felt more like eighteen, the age she was the first time she seduced a man, desperate to shed her virginity like a yoke before she went away to college. Dave had been twenty-nine, separated from his wife, a friend of her older sister's husband. She could tell he was attracted to her so she invited herself to his place, teased him into kissing her after a drink or two and then laid her cards on the table. She actually dangled a maraschino by the stem in front of him and said she wanted to lose her cherry to him. A long, heart-stopping moment passed before he said, in his wise and weary older-man way, "Sure, Isabel, I'd be honored to make love to you."

The memories of what happened then were hazy, like snippets

of a movie all bathed in the golden light of a summer evening: Dave's eyes closing as his lips opened under hers. The lazy glide of his finger between her breasts. The way she'd trembled, as if he'd touched her heart. But she knew better now. Though he'd kissed her breasts and sucked the nipples languidly, sending sweet twinges of pleasure to her pussy, though he'd parted her legs and eased himself into her oh-so-gently, he'd never really touched her. They'd both stayed locked in themselves, Isabel watching and thinking, *Is this fucking—is this all*? Dave moved so slowly, as if enchanted by her, but she realized now it was probably because he was depressed, guilty, confused by his own demons and desires.

There was one moment she treasured, though: the vision of her first lover's face against the pillow as she straddled him, her cunt sliding so easily around him now, her erect, rose-colored nipple dangling before his lips. He looked so happy as he gazed up at her, profoundly content, and her heart soared with the power of it.

Was that what she wanted today? To recapture that power?

Isabel walked up to the reception desk and gave the fresh-faced clerk a smile. Everyone she met seemed so young today, although at second glance, this man was thirtyish, Dave's age back then. She felt a twinge of nostalgic lust.

"I have a reservation for Isabel O'Shea. I was told you could have a room ready for me before the official check-in time."

"Yes, ma'am, it looks like we can do that for you today."

Isabel glanced around the lobby, head held high. Surprisingly enough, at this moment, she felt confident, nothing like people in the movies who were renting their first hotel room for an afternoon's indiscretion.

"How many room keys will you be needing?"

"Two, of course," she replied, leveling her gaze at him.

His eyes flickered. "Certainly, ma'am."

Middle age had its benefits. She'd gotten much better at flirting, especially when it didn't matter, and toying with the clerk was definitely good practice for the real thing. The packet of card keys in hand, she turned and sauntered over to the waiting elevator. A group of businessmen slipped in beside her, three of them, enough to fill the small space with the faint smell of wool, aftershave and male sweat.

Isabel swallowed, her knees weakening from the heady scent. Maybe she should skip the banker and invite this group back to her room? A gang bang—on her terms, of course—was a long-time fantasy. She'd gather them all around her, order them to strip and then feast upon their cocks with her eyes first, comparing the thickness, the curve, the color of the swollen, weeping one-eyed heads. Then she'd take them inside her, one in each hole, willing them to move at her pleasure so she was filled and satisfied, totally, completely and forever.

Do one thing for yourself every day. Simply because you want it.

The elevator stopped at the sixth floor and the men filed out, the last, a curly headed charmer, turning to give her a nod and jaunty smile. *As if he knew.*

Yes, I am a horny trollop planning an afternoon of shameless carnal pleasure with a suit just like you—jealous?

But she didn't say this out loud, of course. She only nodded back with her bookstore owner's smile. It paid to be polite to strangers, who could be potential customers. Isabel had no doubt her business was doing well because of her "nice girl" courtesy, her willingness to take time to cater to her customers' dreams, for that's what a book was—a doorway to another land.

She paused outside the door of room 815. She had a good guess as to what lay on the other side of that doorway. Hotel land. A king-sized bed, a black-and-white art photograph of a city canyon on the wall above it. It was empty now, silent. But later? Would a passing guest hear squeaking bedsprings, male and female grunts and moans as intermingled as their flesh, all the sounds of illicit coupling?

She could only hope.

The room was indeed tasteful, but unremarkable, just as she'd imagined. Unzipping her shoulder bag, she pulled the corset out and laid it out on the bed. It was a whore's corset, red satin trimmed in black lace and scooped low to expose the breasts. Next came the garter belt and the unopened package of silk stockings. Last of all, the condoms, ribbed, for her pleasure.

Which was the purpose of this whole thing anyway.

As she undressed and peeled off her plain, white, married lady's underwear, Isabel couldn't help remembering the first time she and her husband had made love in a hotel. They'd been fucking merrily for almost two years, so she wasn't expecting her wedding night to be a big deal. They'd probably be too tired to do it after the wedding anyway. Her married friends hinted as much.

They were indeed tired, but Isabel wondered, with a poignant smile, if that hotel room was still glowing and throbbing from the incandescent sex they had that night. "It's not like the old days," she'd whispered to him as they fell on the bed together. "I'd have come to you shy and untouched. There's something sexy about having your wedding night be the first time."

He'd smiled and lifted her on top of him. "I'm glad it's not like the old days. Because I know you're going to enjoy it. I know I'm going to make you come."

Which, Isabel had to admit, hadn't happened her real first time. But on her wedding night she did come in a searing, somersaulting rush of sensation she'd never felt before. It was the first time a man ever talked her through it, the forbidden words inflaming her desire as much as the caresses. *I'm going to touch your pussy now. The lips are so swollen and wet. Your clit's hard, like a little diamond. Do you like it, do you like the way I'm rubbing it?*

Yes, oh, yes.

The virgin confession of her lust he'd coaxed from her lips aroused her even more. She began to babble obscene words, she cursed and cried—*Fuck my twat, fuck it hard, oh, god*— dimly wondering how she'd ever managed to be so prim and quiet before. She bellowed like an animal when she came and collapsed in his arms, nearly weeping. Had that silly marriage license, unbelievably, made such a difference? Or was it that they knew, without a doubt, they belonged to each other now?

Was that what she craved today? The surprise? The total abandon?

There wasn't much of that in her life anymore. In many ways, she and her husband were different people now. They led different lives. Isabel's therapist assured her this was very common. Marriage takes work. But in Isabel's eyes, work was the problem. Her husband was a busy, important man. He often traveled and who knew what he did away from home? She never asked. They didn't talk as much as they once had.

How much of it was her doing? Isabel pressed her lips together and banished the prickle of guilt in her belly. After all she'd put up with, he owed her this one transgression. Until now she'd been a good wife. Some might even say she was too accommodating and sweet. Could she be selfish and demanding for a change?

There was a first time for everything.

The banker's admin gave her a broad smile when Isabel walked into the office. Isabel thought she detected a bit of a smirk, but how would the young woman have the faintest idea she was wearing a corset, garters and stockings and no panties under her simple, off-to-the-bank, dark-blue dress? Isabel felt her shoulders tense, her nose wrinkle. She disliked this place and its tinny, impersonal odor of a realm where the lure of money itself won out over any softer, human desire.

Of course, today she was here to change that.

"He can see you now, Ms. O'Shea."

When Isabel opened the door to the inner office, the first thing she saw was the nameplate, ALEXANDER K. TALBOT, resting on his desk like a caption for the man behind it. A perfect banker's name, a perfect banker's face: classic WASP features, overbred blond hair fading to silver at the temples, and of course, the well-tailored suit on that tall body.

She bit back a laugh. This was no time for levity. She had a hotel room waiting.

"The quarterly sales report just came in," Isabel announced, making her voice low and grave.

Alexander K. Talbot frowned. "For the bookstore? Is there a problem?"

"We need to talk."

He cocked his head, his eyes narrowed in concern. Money trouble. She knew that would get his attention. It was time to move in for the kill.

It was easier than she'd thought it would be. That shameless eighteen-year-old adventuress was apparently still alive and well inside her.

Do something selfish. Simply because you want it.

She walked behind the desk and stopped just a few inches from his arm. "Mr. Talbot, do you find me attractive?"

His head snapped back in surprise.

She held her breath. In a moment, everything would be decided.

Then his lips lifted into a smile. He swiveled his chair to face her, his eyes twinkling.

She exhaled.

"Who wouldn't find you attractive?" he said gallantly. "You're a lovely lady."

He probably assumed he could get off with trite flattery, but Isabel pressed on. "I do need to speak with you, Mr. Talbot. Alone. Do you have any important appointments today? Meeting anyone for lunch?"

"No," he replied cautiously.

She pushed the card key across the desk. "Then meet me in room 815 at the Hyatt."

He paused. "All right."

After three days of worrying and plotting, in the end it was as easy as that.

His ready acquiescence made her bolder still. She took his hand in hers and pressed it to her knee. Hands stilled clasped, she helped him slide her dress up over her thigh to the point where the garter belt met the black silk stocking.

He swallowed, staring.

"You will come, won't you?" It was a command more than a question.

"I'll be there. Give me ten minutes."

Isabel dropped his hand, her eye catching the glint of his wedding band. What did that ring mean to him, after all?

She'd find out soon enough.

The sheets had barely warmed around her in the hotel bed when she heard the soft click of the card key in the slot. The door opened. In another moment, her afternoon lover was standing at the foot of the bed, blinking in the dim light, an animal unexpectedly set free from its cage.

"You had something you wanted to discuss?"

She liked the hesitation in his voice. A touch of fear, perhaps? She sat up, revealing her bare breasts and a glimpse of red satin corset. She waited a moment before she spoke, savoring the look of surprise on his face.

"We don't have to talk at all if you'd prefer silence, Mr. Talbot."

"I'll let you decide. It's pretty clear you're the one calling the shots here," he said.

Isabel smiled. Alexander K. Talbot was right. In bed at home—in her ordinary life—she liked to be dominated, although more and more she chafed at such attempts in other parts of the house. But here she was totally in charge, a woman in the prime of life who knew what she wanted and took it. Selfishly. One day at a time.

She stood and walked over to him, her fingers grabbing the lapel of his jacket as she leaned up to kiss him. The cloth was cool and smooth, yet vaguely irritating to her skin. She resisted the urge to tear at it, pull away the shell to uncover the warmer, more vulnerable skin beneath it. She would defile it—and him—in a different way.

"First I want you to turn off your BlackBerry. Then take down your trousers," she said. "I'm going to suck your cock."

His eyebrows shot up. At her tone or the brazen abruptness of the request, she wasn't sure, but he went for his zipper without protest. She watched as he stepped out of his trousers and boxers, privately delighting in the fact he was already hard. For her. Which was foolish because penises were notoriously impersonal in their loyalties. His cock would stand to attention for any female in a red corset, no doubt—his admin, a prostitute, whoever.

"Don't take off the jacket yet."

He stopped, hands on his lapels, and immediately dropped his arms to his sides as if to await her next command.

She knelt to take his bobbing erection in her mouth. It tasted…different. Faintly bitter, smelling like money, and yet it was a flavor she craved. It was the first time she'd ever sucked off a man wearing a jacket and tie and the perversity of it spurred her on to a new vigor, lapping and circling the head with her tongue, gripping the base with her hand. She swallowed him and began to hum.

"Jesus," he whispered, his hand, the one with the wedding band, stroking her hair.

She pulled away. "Do you like that?"

"Yes. Very much." His hand brushed the corset. "I like this. Where did you get it?"

She sat back on her heels and gazed up at him. He towered over her, and by all rights, it should have been a submissive position, but, oddly, it didn't feel that way today.

"No questions from you, Mr. Talbot. Just answers. Are you telling me that you are glad you took time off from your esteemed job at one of our nation's finest banks to do naughty things with a hussy like me?"

"I can't deny it," he replied, his lips twitching.

"Then we'll proceed. Take off your jacket. Not the shirt or the tie. I want you wearing them while we fuck."

His brow creased in a faint frown. Naturally, a fastidious banker would be worried about a mess on his nice, proper uniform.

"I won't get them dirty. Just a bit of pussy juice on the shirttails maybe. You won't mind a little souvenir of me, will you?"

A smile playing on his lips, he shook his head obediently and took off his jacket, tossing it over the desk chair.

"Good boy. Before you put it inside, though, I want you to lick me. With proper deference. Get on your hands and knees, please."

The smile shifted back to surprise, but he did as he was told.

Isabel sat at the edge of the bed and parted her legs. The garter straps tightened over her thighs, dark against her pale skin. "Come here. Let's see how wet you can make me."

His cheeks were flushed now as he crawled the three steps to her, his tie dragging on the carpet. If only the bank president could see him now.

Positioning himself between her thighs, he looked up, as if for a sign to begin. Isabel nodded. His tongue darted out, teasing her clit with quick little flicks.

She closed her eyes. She had to get past the strangeness, the chill of this anonymous room, the unusual position, the glint of bright noon sun peeking through the window.

The warm tongue shifted its rhythm now, circling her pleasure spot with a slow stirring motion she loved. Her breath came faster and her thighs began to shake. She was melting, melting into the sheets, her belly humming. She'd crossed over, to that place where nothing else mattered but this hot, pulsing sensation between her legs. A few more flicks of that tongue and she might take the final step, up and over the edge.

But that's not how she wanted it to end.

"Stop. Right now," she barked.

He pulled away. She opened her eyes to study him, to see if he had changed. His mouth glistened, his eyes were glazed. He'd crossed over, too.

"Lie on the bed."

Without a word, he followed her instructions.

She sat herself down beside his outstretched body, solicitously, as if she were nursing him for the flu. "Do you have a condom with you?"

He looked confused. "Why do you ask?"

"Because a bad boy like you who fucks naughty sluts on his

lunch hour needs to remember to wear a condom. You don't want to take anything nasty home with you, do you?"

He stared at her, speechless. But Isabel figured she had to allow for that. All the blood had gone to his dick, after all.

"Fortunately I happen to have brought one along for you. Smart businesswomen have to plan ahead."

"Yes, they do," he agreed, watching docilely as she ripped open the condom wrapper and rolled it on him. How many years had it been since she'd done this? Then she remembered, with a pang of selfishness, that it would certainly save her some mess in the end.

"Listen carefully," she cooed as she swung her leg over his belly and positioned his cockhead at her opening. "I'm going to ask you to do a little multitasking now, Mr. Talbot. I'm sure your demanding job has trained you well for that. I'll sit here, still and quiet, while you suck one nipple—the right one—and play with the other one with your left hand. With your right hand, I'd like you to tease my asshole, nice and slow, until I come on your cock."

His cock twitched in her hand and he made a funny sound in his throat.

"Is that amenable to you, sir?"

"I believe so," he said, his voice hoarse.

"Then go to it."

Just as instructed, he leaned up and took her nipple in his mouth. His left hand tweaked the other nipple, sending sizzling jolts straight to her pussy. Still and quiet, that's what she'd promised, but in spite of herself, Isabel squirmed, instinctively grinding her clit into him. There was nothing strange or new about this. The pleasure of this dance was profoundly familiar, timeless. His right hand circled around to her back, gliding along her spine to the furrow of her buttocks. One finger delved lower, soft and teasing. She felt a cry rising in her throat, but she held it back. Still and quiet, that's what she'd be. But when he found her hole, circling the exquisitely sensitive ring of muscles as if he were stroking a pet, her cunt muscles convulsed around him and she groaned. Loudly.

Fuck my twat. Fuck it hard.

He arched up to meet her in perfect response to her own desperate thrusts. He was a fine multitasker indeed—sucking, tweaking, teasing hands and cock and tongue working all at once. And she was working, too, slamming her clit against his belly, arching her back to offer her breasts for more. She couldn't be still or silent; it was all too hot, too much. She felt the heat gathering in her belly, shooting up her spine, exploding from her throat in a hoarse scream.

Fuck, I'm coming, oh, god.

He followed behind her, his fingers and tongue still working diligently as her contractions faded. Only a soft, rhythmic grunting and the slower, deeper glide of his thrusts told her he'd shot his wad into that condom.

Her chest still heaving, she opened her eyes and gazed down at him. He looked good, his flushed face framed by the pure white of the pillow. He smiled. She smiled back.

They weren't strangers anymore.

That was the real reason she'd done this. Simply that. Isabel realized it now.

"Jesus, that was hot, Izzy," he said.

"I'm glad you enjoyed it, Alex, my dear," she replied with a saucy smile.

He rolled the condom in a tissue and tossed it in the trash can by the bed. "I haven't worn one of these in twenty years."

"I'm glad to hear that," she said, snuggling against him. "It was so easy luring you away from your office, I wondered if you were such a soft touch with all the women who are hard up for a loan."

"Only ones wearing red corsets. Rest assured, this is the first time I've ever done something like this."

"It's part of Tracy's assignment, you know. And you thought it just meant you had to do the dishes."

"I'm starting to think this therapy thing was a good idea after all." His smile faded. "By the way, is there a problem with finances at the store?"

She laughed. "Actually, we're doing very well."

"That's because you're such a good boss."

"Just good?" she said. "I'd say fucking amazing."

Her cocky reply slipped out before she could stop herself. She'd never bragged about her management skills so openly before. But the gleam in Alex's eyes told her he very much approved.

It was yet another first time today. She had a feeling she could get used to this.

AIR-CONDITIONING. COLOR TV. LIVE MERMAIDS

Anna Meadows

He first saw her through the glass, turning in the water so her hair whipped behind her. She'd grown it out. It billowed and rippled to her waist. It must have taken her an hour a night to comb it. She never used to let it grow past her shoulders, or the Santa Anas would tangle it so bad she couldn't even get it into two braids. He'd never told her how much he liked it that way, all wild and weedy from crawling through the grass to catch ladybugs or spinning on the tire swing. He'd watched her from the tree house then, her hair fanning out like black sea oats.

He knew the shape of her body, not so different from the summer they graduated high school. She had that same softness in her thighs—he could see that even through the mermaid tail, covered in sequins the color of a peacock. But if he didn't know her by her body, he would have known her by how her hair spread out in the water, the same way it did in the pond back home, like she was falling.

"House beer's half off," the bartender said. "Looks like you need it."

Daniel ordered one but didn't drink it. He was still watching her.

He'd been on his way home to visit family for the holiday weekend when he saw the sign on the side of the highway. MERMAID MOTEL. HOME OF DIVE IN THE DESERT. AIR-CONDITIONING. COLOR TV. LIVE MERMAIDS. He turned off and got a room—he was tired enough that if he stopped, it'd have to be for the night—because the last two words on the sign made him think of Lila, turning underwater in the pond.

"One day I'm gonna be a mermaid," she'd said every time she came up for air. She always had on a one-piece, because her mother never let her wear anything else. "Only *putas* wear those two-pieces," Mrs. Ramirez would call out the window as they got on their bikes. It just made Daniel want Lila more, thinking of her belly staying pale as her shoulders browned. Her costume at Dive in the Desert may have been her first two-piece, a bra so heavy with teal rhinestones it flattened her breasts, and a mermaid tail with a fin so big that carrying it around must've tired her out by the end of her shift.

Dive in the Desert was the bar in the downstairs of the Mermaid Motel, fifty-nine dollars a night, and that was in the high season. The filled seats in the bar usually numbered more than twice the daily check-ins at the Mermaid. The bar was on the trucking highway, the Ocean Floor Onion Rings were supposed to be the best in the state, and when a mermaid came out, the house beer was half off. The owner once had big plans, a nightly show with a half-dozen mermaids all flicking their tails at the long-haul truckers. But after he got the kitchen up to code, he only had enough money left for a secondhand aquarium, just big enough for one mermaid, two if one of them was Lila. She was so short that she fit in the tank with one of the other girls. That was why the owner had hired her, even though she had little boobs and her hair hadn't quite been long enough at the time.

"It'll grow," Lila had said, standing in his office in her jean shorts and a ten-year-old T-shirt from the Grand Canyon. "My hair, I mean."

Lila was still learning, but now she knew how to flip in the tank, twisting her hips like the older mermaids taught her. "It makes all the little jewels get the light," Yolanda had said. Lila was usually with one of them—she was good at getting out of the way, even with that big tail—but today she was on her own. The other mermaids had family to see for the holiday weekend, and while most places got booked up, nobody was making the drive to the middle of the Mojave to check in to the Mermaid Motel. Even the long-haul truckers went home if they could get the time off. The bar would be almost empty if it weren't for families making pit stops on road trips to somewhere else. The bar was getting more orders for grilled cheese sandwiches than gin and tonics. The little girls came up to the tank and pointed, and the boys tapped on the glass like Lila was a fish. She waved as she swam past, blowing a kiss with a string of little air bubbles.

Through the glass, she saw a man standing by himself at the other side of the bar, as far as he could get from the tank and still watch her. He had hair the color of the *masa de harina* Lila and her mother used to mix with water to make corn tortillas. He was about the right age, twenty-five or so, same as her, but she knew it wasn't Daniel. She'd thought she'd seen him at least ten times since she started at Dive in the Desert. Every time a young-looking guy with hair the color of sand-soil showed up in jeans, she'd see the blur of him through the water and the glass, and she'd think it was him. But every time she surfaced enough to peek over the edge of the tank, she was wrong. By now she'd given up looking and didn't come up until she needed the air so much her lungs grew tight in her rib cage.

The ketchup-and-french-fry crowd thinned out. Her shift ended. She rinsed off at the showerhead behind the bar, shielded by stacks of old crates. She left the costume on to rinse it out, the fin folded under her feet. Her eyes stung with the salt, and the turquoise sky blurred into the terra-cotta of the desert.

She shut off the water. Her vision was still a little fuzzy, but not enough that she didn't notice the man standing just on the other side of the crates. She startled. It wasn't the first time a drunk man had tried to watch one of the mermaids rinse the smell of the tank out of her hair, but they were usually looking for Sarah Jane, with that hair so blonde it looked white in the light of the tank, or Yolanda, with her breasts that spilled into her sequined bra like batter into a muffin tin.

Lila held her hands over her costume top. "Get out of here."

"All right," the man said. "But I'm waiting you out. I'll be in the lobby."

She recognized the voice, a little lower than she remembered, but with the same slow, even rhythm.

She rubbed her eyes to get the last of the salt out. "Daniel?"

The shape of him came into focus, a Polaroid developing. He had his hands in the pockets of his jeans, like always. Without pockets, he never knew what to do with them.

She laughed, and he slipped in between the stacks of crates and put his arms around her, like he would with a friend he hadn't seen in a while. But it didn't feel right. He and Lila had never been that way.

"What are you doing here?" she asked.

"Just stopped for the night," he said.

"Nobody stops here unless they get a flat or an overheated radiator."

She smelled like rock salt and desert and sky, a scent that was waiting on her skin when they were growing up, but now was as strong as open lilies.

She held her hand to the front of his shirt, damp now, and sticking to him. "I'm getting you wet," she said, and laughed again.

"I don't care." He held her again, but this time her mouth ended up on the patch of his shirt just over his collarbone. Her wet fingers pulled down the collar of his shirt, and she put her lips to the base of his neck.

She took in the scent of him. He still smelled like wet grass, like he slept in it every night. She stood on her toes to move her lips up his neck, the balls of her feet gripping the ground through the fabric of her tail. She tasted the light dusting of salt that perspiration had left on his skin. His hands gripped her waist, and he stopped holding her like a sister or an old friend.

He picked her up like she was something strange and pretty he'd found on a beach hundreds of miles from the desert. She put her arms around him, feeling the warmth of his back through his shirt, and kissed the rest of the salt off his neck. Her tail dripped on the asphalt and then the dry dirt parking lot. When the sun hit those tacky little rhinestones, they shimmered on her body like malachite. The men getting some air outside the bar were too drunk to notice, the women at the motel check-in desk too bored. A girl on the way to the car with her family pointed and said she saw the mermaid, but her mother didn't look, and said no, the mermaids were inside in the water where they could breathe.

The door to Daniel's room fell shut behind them, and he laid her down on the bed. Her hair and her tail soaked the sheets, and the whole room smelled like salt water. He helped her wriggle out of her tail and freed her breasts from her costume top. She'd wanted to be a mermaid worse than anything else since she was five years old, but right now shedding the weight of all those sequins made her feel like he'd woken her body up from a spell made of blue light and a shimmer of green. Like having his hands on her damp skin had turned her naked and human so she could part her legs.

She pulled his jeans down only as far as she needed to, and she slid under him. He hesitated, sure she couldn't mean for him to do that. He'd brought her back to his room to see her and touch her, to check her face and body against his memory and make sure he had it all right. But she put her hand on his back to tell him that, yes, this was what she wanted.

The soft ache of opening for him had the feel and color of something she wanted to taste, so much so that she almost made him pull out of her so she could put her mouth around his erection. She didn't. Instead she dug her heels into his lower back. He was gentle and slow, like she always guessed he would be. She loved that about him, like she loved how his hands were always in his pockets and how his hair was always just long enough to get in his eyes. But it made her so impatient she wrapped her legs around him tighter, lifting her butt and the small of her back up off the bed and closer to him so he was all the way inside her before he meant to be.

He caught a gasp in the back of his throat. She kissed him, and he eased her lips apart with his tongue. He was still inside her, but they laughed softly, just breathing, no real sound, because it was the first time they'd kissed since he'd shown up. It was the only part of it all that they'd done before, and they both wondered how they could've gotten so far without their lips touching.

She tightened around him, and they couldn't laugh anymore. The muscles inside her tensed and released, a rhythm she couldn't help, and he couldn't help finishing. His hand was already between her legs by the time he did. He traced his fingers around the little slick-wet pearl that made her thighs tremble the more he touched it. He couldn't remember when he started thinking of it that way, as her pearl. It was years before he ever touched it, years after the first time she said she wanted to be a mermaid, maybe sometime the summer after high school when she lived in that black one-piece. It had been strapless, her mother's one concession about swimsuits, so he'd been able to watch Lila's shoulders darken over those months.

Lila curled onto her side, pleasure blooming between her legs. At first she tried not to scream, then she remembered that nobody was out at the Mermaid Motel on a holiday weekend. The rooms on either side of Daniel's were probably empty. She let herself, and she could feel the shiver that her cry sent through him.

He held her as her breathing evened. She wondered if she should say thank you when a man made her feel like that, the same as if he held a door open or remembered what kind of *chiles* she liked.

Daniel kissed her back and caught the faint scent of the water in the tank. "Salt," he said. "Not chlorine?"

"Salt's cheaper," she said.

The hum of the air conditioner mixed with the sound of the ice machine turning over. It was a little like the buzz of the generator boxes and telephone lines in the neighborhood where they'd grown up.

"How'd you find me?" she asked.

"You were always saying you wanted to be a mermaid," he said. "How come you didn't tell me where you were going? One day I called and your mom just said you'd moved out."

The ice machine died down, but the air conditioner still called up the memory of lawn sprinklers. They'd talked about going to a hotel together, one day when they were older, but they'd meant one in the city, one nice enough that they didn't put VACANCY and PAY-PER-VIEW on their signs. But lying with him like this was putting Lila a little more on the side of cheap places with neon sides and bars next door.

"Why've you been hiding?" he asked.

"You were in college," she said. "Was I supposed to think you'd come back?"

"Yes," he said. He never had asked her why she didn't try going too. He'd always had two guesses and didn't like either one. Maybe she didn't have the money and didn't apply for scholarships. "We don't take charity from *los gringos*," her mother always told her. Or maybe it was because Mrs. Ramirez was always saying that girls shouldn't get too smart. But by then it was already too late for that. Lila was always smarter than Daniel and everybody else. She'd figured out how to lock her bedroom door with a skein of yarn and a few hairpins. She'd sewn old textbooks back together when the ones the school handed out were so worn the pages were falling out. That was how he knew, when she said she'd be a mermaid one day, that she'd do it.

"How long are you here for?" she asked.

He interlaced his fingers with hers and kissed the back of her hand. "I don't know," he said. "You tell me."

She reached behind her, her fingers tracing a path from his chest down to his crotch. He responded before she even touched him. She laughed in that way that scared him but always got him a little harder. Her costume, spread out on the floor like a skin she'd molted out of, caught the last of the afternoon sun through the blinds and cast comet trails of blue-green light on her body, still pale from the water. A girl turning under the surface of a pond, a woman in the coarse sheets and ice-machine white noise of a desert motel.

PROOF OF DESIRE

Remittance Girl

The lobby at the Russell Hotel in Bloomsbury was a poem to Victorian monstrosities, but the room itself was simply chilly and beige. It smelled faintly of stale cigarette smoke and carpet shampoo. Beyond the open curtains, the streetlamps were splayed in the cold, winter air. From her place in the nondescript beige armchair, Emma thought the man on the bed looked vulnerable. Lit by the gloom of the bedside lamps, Sean lay with his back propped against the padded headboard, lanky legs stretched out in front of him. His shoes and socks were off, and his jeans were unbuttoned, the fly open to his purpose. His fist stroked the pale column of his erect cock.

"Is this all you want?" His words were hesitant but heavy with breath.

A lie of a nod and a tight smile; of course it wasn't all she wanted. What she wanted was to dispense with her panties, climb onto the bed and sink down onto his cock. But that wasn't going to happen. That she wouldn't allow herself and she had told him so.

"Are you sure?" Sean's hand made slick sounds as it moved over his oiled erection.

Evening traffic noise from outside seeped through the closed windows. Somewhere in the distance someone was breaking glass. "Yes. I'm sure. Just what we agreed on. Okay?"

He stopped, fingers cupping the engorged head. His thumb brushed the blunted tip. "I thought maybe you'd change your mind. You know, when you got here. Once we actually met."

She'd worried about the same thing. She'd watched many, many men do this, witnessed many couples fuck in settings just like this one, but never with a friend. Never someone she felt any affection for. Now, there in that purgatory of a room, she wondered if she'd made a mistake.

"Don't be hurt, Sean. I told you it would be like this. I can't help the way I am."

"I know. I just thought…"

She smiled again—it took more of an effort this time—and shook her head. "Please, just…come for me. That's all."

His throat was dry as he swallowed. She heard the effort of it above the ambient noise of the room. He glanced down at his crotch and began to masturbate again, not with much enthusiasm.

"Talk to me, then. It feels sterile with you just sitting there."

Her mouth crooked. This time it was effortless. "But you're hard anyway, aren't you?"

"My dick is stupid. But I'm not. Talk to me. Please."

She knew what he wanted, the things that got him off. She'd typed them often enough. But saying it aloud—that was harder. Nonetheless, she owed him that much. Closing her eyes, she took a deep breath and then began.

"You're such a slut, Sean. Such a filthy, dirty slut. Stroking your cock in some shabby, anonymous hotel room for a woman you've never met in your life."

He let out a jagged whisper of a breath. It ended in a little whine. His hand began to move again, circled thumb and fingers tightening, pulling up and down on the skin of the shaft.

"You're hard. So fucking hard," she let her tone drop, "and you just can't help yourself, can you? So filthy."

A groan wormed up from somewhere deep in his throat, the slick sounds grew louder, faster.

"That's it. Just like that. You love it, don't you? Showing me just what a piece of cunt toy you are? All you want to do is come. But don't you dare do it without my permission." She injected a level of menace into the last of her words. "Don't you dare."

"Please...don't," he stammered. His eyes slid closed as his fist worked harder.

She felt better now that his eyes were shut. She pushed herself out of the chair. "Don't? Don't what?" Her voice descended to an almost whisper as she approached the bed. "Look at you. Degenerate. That's what you are. And you can't help yourself, can you?"

"No." The word was strangled by arousal.

The imagery didn't turn her on. She'd never been all that interested in dominating men. But his reaction to her words, the lust they invoked, tightened her chest, made her belly flutter.

"Fuck, I should tie you to the bed, pillows piled under your hips until your shameless ass is as high as I want it. And then fuck you till you scream."

Sean let out a choked groan. He was pumping furiously now. Pearls of precome teared from the tip. The droplets landed, with each stroke, on his bare white stomach, catching and glistening in the darker hairs that ran up to his navel.

When she reached the bed, she bent over, leaning on her

hands as she brought her mouth closer to his ear. "I'd use you like a hole," she growled. "Like the slutty, wanton little cunt you are."

"God. Fuck me. Please."

There it was. Need, desire so strong it burst into the stillness of the room, tainting the air with an ache. It hurt. It hurt deliciously to stand so close, to see the beads of sweat that birthed and glinted along the line of his sternum. To smell the faded scent of morning soap rise off his skin, and the sweetness of the oil he'd used on his cock, and the richer musk of his crotch. The tip of her tongue prickled with want. Her cunt felt swollen, sticky. Afterward, alone, she'd take care of it.

"Fuck you? Are you mad? I wouldn't fucking touch you. I wouldn't sully my skin with you. I'd use a dildo."

"No," he whimpered. "No. Ride me. I want you on me, around me."

"Never. I don't fuck trash like you."

His eyes flew open and he turned his head toward her. "Then kiss me. Kiss me."

Something in his voice had changed. He'd broken the spell. He'd cheated. A scythe-like blade of ice pushed into her gut. She pulled back.

"No."

"Yes! Please!"

His hand shot out, fingers surrounding one of her wrists. It was the hand he'd used to stroke his cock, slick with oil and hot with friction. She tugged against the grip that held, then slipped, then held again, suddenly terrified.

"Stop it. Let go, Sean."

"Just a kiss. Just one." He was on his knees, free hand curling around the back of her neck to pull her toward him, a desperate uncontrolled urgency in the embrace.

"No. Don't...don't spoil this," she said more softly, making her voice gentle, tamping down her own panic. Her gaze held his and she furrowed her brow. "Don't ruin everything."

The hold on her neck eased and he freed her wrist, leaving the smear of oil and heat behind. "Jesus. I'm sorry."

She knew better than to draw away just then. Instead she sat down on the side of the bed, smoothing her skirt over her thighs. "I'm sorry, too. It's not your fault. I shouldn't have asked you to do this."

"No. I said I could do it. I said I wanted to. It's my fault."

The fingers, still resting lightly on her neck, moved. His thumb caressed the tendon there. The sensation, no matter how sweet, how well meaning, was too much. Too tender. Too intimate. It was breaking her heart.

She shook her head and smiled at the wall. Tears pricked at her eyes. "Don't apologize. It's fine." Carefully pulling his hand off her neck, she laid it on the bed and patted it. "I should go."

"Don't. I can do this. I said I could, and I can. Do you still want me to?"

"I'm not sure."

"Please. We'll start again."

It had already gone too far, too wrong. Part of her wanted to get out of that fucking hotel room as quick as she could and drink herself into enough of a stupor to fall asleep. But the other part—the better part, she thought—didn't want to hurt him.

"All right." She gave him a quick smile and got to her feet.

"Can't you just sit here, a little closer? It helps."

She thought for a moment, feeling blindly for her limitations, and then sat back down. "Okay, but don't touch me. Can you do that?"

Sean cocked his head. "Yes. I guess. I don't understand why not. I wouldn't force you, you know. I'd never do that."

"I know. Just…please don't touch me. Touch yourself."

He worried his lip. "Okay. But look at me. Talk to me."

"What do you want me to say? Do you want me to talk the way we do online?"

Shifting back on the bed, settling back against the headboard, he exhaled. "No, just…just tell me what you want."

"I want to watch you feel pleasure."

A smile bent the edge of his mouth; his hand returned to his cock. It was semierect and gave a little bob as he touched it. "What else?"

"I want to listen as the arousal begins to take you over."

He began to stroke again, slowly and deliberately. It only took three or four to regain his erection. He glanced from her, down to his groin, then back again. "What else?" he repeated.

"I want to see you come."

"Why?"

"Because it's proof. Proof of pleasure."

He was looking into her eyes now, fist moving faster. Little twitches tugged at the muscles of his jaw. "Know what I want?"

"Not really. Tell me."

"I want to know what you taste like. Whether it's like I imagined."

She smiled. "What else?"

"I want…" His breath came quicker now, lips parted between his words. "To feel your lips around my cock. The heat, the pressure of them."

"My mouth? Wet? Tight?"

"Yes. Sucking. With my fingers in your hair."

Her nipples stung as they stiffened. She fought not to break eye contact with him, but his gaze was starving her of oxygen. "What else?"

"Then to kiss you. And taste my cock on your mouth."

"Not come in it?"

"No," he rasped. "No, against you. On your skin."

The ache in her cunt turned to sharp needles as the muscles fluttered. A single hot surge of wetness soaked her panties. "Where?"

Sean squeezed his cock, pumping it steadily. "Your skin."

"But where?"

"Your breasts…belly…thighs…I'd paint you."

"Why?"

"Because."

"Because why?"

"I'm close. Very close." His jaw trembled as he spoke. The sinews on his throat stood out against his skin.

"I know. Come for me."

Sean took one enormous breath and held it. His eyes turned sightless as the orgasm overloaded his synapses. She glanced down. A pale stream of come spattered his stomach, and then another, and another.

The familiar surge of sharp-edged elation swept over her body, setting her skin aflame, making her heart pound against her rib cage. Then, after a few moments, she looked up and smiled.

"Well, that worked," he muttered.

"Yes, it did. Thank you."

"Oh, no. Thank you." He gave a little chuckle. "So, would it kill you to kiss me now?"

She stood up. The chemicals made it impossible for her to stop smiling. They fizzled in her veins like soda, her pulse almost deafening in her ears. She picked up her purse, avoiding his gaze.

"Yes, it would."

She left the room, shutting the door quietly behind her.

SOUNDPROOF

Emily Moreton

The thing with cheap hotels was that the sitcom couple next door getting it on too loudly had a tendency to become a reality. Even more so when the cheap hotel was really more of a converted house and the only room available was a single with the bed tucked up against the adjoining—and not well sound-proofed—wall.

The first night hadn't been too bad; Led Zeppelin wasn't the easiest thing to fall asleep to, but Sam had managed it, focusing on the rhythm of the music instead of the rhythm of the bedsprings. Problem was, it turned out iPods weren't as durable as he'd always been told, or at least they weren't durable enough to survive an unexpected dunking when he'd lost his footing in the sand, soaking his jeans and the music player in his pocket.

Actually, the rhythmic creaking springs were sort of hypnotic if he focused on the sound and not the meaning behind it. Eyes closed, hands folded neatly over his bare stomach, cool summer breeze blowing in through the open window, he could almost—

The girl moaned, loud and high pitched, and Sam cursed, dragging the pillow from behind his head and pressing it over his ears, where it did approximately fuck-all to block out the sound.

At least someone was having a good time. So was he, during the day, climbing the 199 steps to Whitby Abbey, sketching on the beach with the sand between his toes and generally enjoying being alone and away from the office for a few days.

Or he would be, if he could get some sleep. He knew he should get up, knock and tell them to shut up, but he was comfortable, nestled just right on the slightly lumpy mattress, and if he got up, he'd have to put on some kind of clothes and the whole thing just felt like too much trouble.

How much longer could they really go on, anyway?

The rhythm of the bedsprings sped up, the girl's voice, half muffled through the wall, half drifting in through the open window, went high and breathless, "Oh, oh, oh, yes, yes, oh, yes," and even Sam wanted to shudder when she trailed off.

Instead, he smiled up at the dark ceiling and closed his eyes, anticipating pleasant dreams, followed by a day out in the bay fishing.

He was nearly asleep when the girl's voice, sounding like she stood right by his bed, said, "Again?"

"No," Sam said firmly, half hoping they'd hear him. "Not again. You need your beauty sleep, and these aren't the newest beds in the world. Who even knows if they can stand up to this kind of strenuous use?"

Apparently they didn't care, judging from the flurry of squeaking, followed by the guy's low, pleased moan.

Sam didn't even know what they looked like—unsurprisingly, they didn't seem to be early risers—but he was hit suddenly by the image of a young man on his back, his partner climbing on top of him, swinging one tan, smooth leg over him and sinking down onto his cock. Sam's mind helpfully added in the guy's hand on his dick, holding it steady for the girl, and apparently the guy was dark-haired, the girl's hair so pale blonde it was almost white, both of them slim and fit.

His own cock twitched with interest in the picture, or maybe in the soundtrack. The bedsprings were squeaking in a slower rhythm now. The man in Sam's head was rolling his hips up, his hands on the girl's waist as she rocked with his rhythm.

Sam's cock twitched again. He pressed both hands firmly to his stomach, opening his eyes to look up at the dark ceiling. It wasn't right—they didn't know he was listening, wouldn't know what he was doing. It was kind of creepy to be getting off on someone else having sex, especially sex that they probably wouldn't consent to him listening in on.

On the other hand, it wasn't like he'd consented to being invited into their sex life by having to listen to it, and if they couldn't keep it down in a hotel, they had only themselves to blame.

Plus, it wasn't like they'd ever know.

Sam ran one hand lightly down his stomach and over his cock, rocking his hips up to nudge the head against his cupped palm. It felt good, even though he was only halfway to hard.

The guy next door apparently thought the same thing, from the low groan he gave, his voice hoarse. "You feel so good," Sam heard through the wall.

Sam would just bet she did—and clearly, it had been way too long since he'd had sex. He stroked himself more firmly, awkward and rough without anything to slick the way, but like hell was he getting up to ferret in his shaving kit for lube. He rubbed his thumb lightly over the head of his cock, swallowing his own groan at how good that felt. Never mind it being too long since he'd had sex; it had clearly been way too long since he'd even spent enough time getting himself off.

"...So hot like that," the guy said, the first few words lost to the wall and a sudden swirl of breeze catching at the curtains. He could have meant anything; the version of him in Sam's head meant the way his partner was cupping her right breast in her hand, working at the nipple with her thumb, flashes of hard, pink flesh as she moved her hand.

Sam stroked his hand up his stomach and over his chest, catching his thumb on his own nipple, caught between imagining someone else's hand on him, and imagining it was his hand on someone else's body, someone else's nipple peaking against the pad of his thumb. The way his ragged nail caught on his chest hair, the lack of soft curves, it still worked for him— for all his lack of application lately, Sam was equal opportunity about his sex partners.

He kept his eyes closed, concentrating on how the bedsprings were getting another workout, the occasional thump of the headboard against the wall. Maybe the guy would like it if Sam crawled into the bed with them, got his mouth on the guy's nipple. Sam pinched his own, not as good as the sharp nip of teeth, but close, as close as he was going to get like this. The thumb he was rubbing over the head of his cock was damp now, precome smearing slick and messy over hot skin. Sam slid his cupped palm over his cock, moaning a little at how good it felt, then stroked himself, and god, that was better, that was so much better. Slick and hot and wet, it felt so good.

He rocked his hips up, catching the rhythm of the couple next door, who'd sped up considerably. For a moment, Sam thought of the last time he'd been in a hotel, a weekend away with a friend with benefits who'd taken forever to get her first orgasm, then gone off with almost nothing for three or four after.

Inviting a mutual friend to join them had been a great idea; Sam would give them a call when he got back to London, see if they wanted to hook up.

He wasn't entirely surprised to blink his eyes open for a moment, and find, when he closed them again, that the anonymous couple had turned into Wei and Jess. Jess didn't have the perfect tan and toned body of his hypothetical girl, but watching her, half memory, half fantasy, made Sam's cock jerk in his hand.

He could hear himself breathing, too loud, too fast, almost panting, a sharp burst of sound coming from his throat on every exhalation. Next door, the girl was gasping out sharp, "Ah, ah, ah," noises in time with the headboard knocking at the wall, and then said, "Put your—touch me," and Sam thought for a second that he'd come just from that, from imagining Wei's hand between Jess's legs, his own hand between the anonymous girl's legs; how she'd feel, slick and wet on his fingers as he rubbed at her, how her voice would—did—go high pitched, sharp and loud, too loud, god, she sounded—

"Not yet, not yet, I'm close, don't," the guy said. Sam worked his own cock hard, fucking up into his own fist, twisting a little over the head, his thumb on that spot that felt so good. He brought his free hand down to cup his balls, rolling them in his palm, damp with sweat, desperate to get there before they did.

"Oh, fuck," the girl shouted, "oh, fuck, don't stop, don't stop, don't stop don't stop, don't—"

Her shout of pleasure couldn't really be misinterpreted, even if it hadn't been followed by a cessation of all thumping and squeaking. Sam kept up his own rhythm for a handful of strokes, reaching for his climax, but it was already starting to back off, the intensity he'd felt a moment ago dissipating.

He slowed down, catching his breath. He'd kicked the covers

off at some point, and the sheet under his back was damp with his own sweat. From the room next door, he could hear murmuring voices—great, the exchange of sweet nothings part of the evening.

The last thing he was expecting was the thump-squeak of bodies changing position, followed by the girl's voice moaning and the guy's dragging low in a long exhalation of pure pleasure. Surely they couldn't be—she'd sounded totally done with that orgasm—but the man's voice sounded questioning, followed by hers assenting.

Jess, sprawled naked on her back, Wei sliding into her, her hands curled tight around the headboard, his on her shoulders holding her in place as he fucked her, driving toward his orgasm.

Sam moaned, speeding up the strokes to his own cock, his heartbeat picking up as he got his climax back in sight. Distantly, he was aware that he was moaning again, too loud, that his own bedsprings were squeaking as he jerked his hips up into his own hand. None of it mattered—he was pretty sure he couldn't have stopped for anything short of a fire alarm, and then only if it was accompanied by an actual fire.

The guy cried out, "Yes, yes, yes, oh, god," and Sam slammed his hand down on his cock as he shoved his hips up one more time, and came all over himself.

He slept through breakfast the next morning, and woke up too hot, skin grubby with dried sweat and come, thigh muscles aching. Totally worth it. He hadn't passed out after coming since he was a teenager getting sucked off for the first time.

He wasn't going to make the fishing trip he'd idly thought about joining. Standing in the shower, he decided he could still go out on the pier, where he'd seen fishermen the day before. A day doing nothing much would be good after the night before.

He should have expected it, but his life, the night before notwithstanding, wasn't a sitcom or a farce. Upon opening his door to find his next door neighbor—the woman, who was shorter than he'd imagined her, and a little older, dark hair cut short around her ears—stepping out of hers, he immediately felt his face go bright red.

"Good morning," he said, hoping she'd attribute the rasp in his voice to—well, anything really, anything that wasn't, *I'm embarrassed because I listened to you fuck last night and I'd totally do you now that I've seen you.*

She smiled, showing crooked teeth. "I was hoping I might run into you. Um." She looked both ways down the corridor like she was hoping for salvation, then met his eyes again when it failed to materialize. "I don't want to, um, police your sexuality or anything, and I think it's great that you're so…open…about sex, especially when you're, you know, on your own—not that there's anything wrong with masturbating, I mean, everyone does it… Right. It's just—you were kind of loud? Last night?" She giggled a little. "Walls are thin, you know, and don't get me wrong, it sounded like you were having a great time, but we'd just sort of prefer not to be, you know, part of it."

Sam closed his mouth, which he was pretty sure had fallen open when she started talking about masturbation. Tempting as it was to point out that he'd never have started anything if she and her partner had kept it down to a dull roar, it was clear that she had no idea he'd been able to hear them (how was that even possible, what, they thought they were quiet? Maybe they fucked with earplugs in). "I'll try," he promised, hoping he wasn't still blushing. Actually, what the hell, if he was going to be uncomfortable, she could be as well. "Maybe I'll dig out that gag."

She blinked, her eyes hot. "That always works for me,"

she said. "Anyway, Jake's waiting for me; nice to meet you. In person, as it were."

"You, too," Sam said automatically, and waited until she'd turned the corner before he thumped his head back against his own door. He was so screwed, and totally not in the good way.

Well, unless he could persuade her that gags could work for the three of them together. Sam headed toward the lifts, already plotting out the coming night's entertainment.

AN INSPECTOR COMES

Suzanne Fox

The Art Nouveau decor of the country house whisked me back to 1930s England, an era of decadent sophistication. Why was I here? I had asked myself this question all the way to the hotel. After all, I was about to spend the next two days in the company of strangers while trying to solve a pretend murder.

It was Gavin's fault. He's the brother of one of my friends and he loves murder mysteries, trying to convert everyone he meets into becoming an amateur sleuth. After months of his enthusiastic tales, I finally submitted to his sales pitch and booked a place on the Manor Hotel's murder weekend. I suppose I was intrigued and even looking forward to dressing up in the clothing of the period, imagining what it was like to be one of the privileged few who behaved badly without responsibility.

I was shown to my room by Robert, dressed in the maroon uniform of a 1930s bellhop. There the decor continued with beautiful, carved oak furniture and sumptuous, deep red, soft furnishings. It was a luxurious change from my minimalist apartment.

After unpacking, I studied the itinerary that I'd received earlier. The instructions were brief. I was Coco Devine, a wealthy socialite, and I was to dress accordingly. The party would consist of a mixture of paying guests, plus a number of actors who would mingle with the party. Drinks and introductions were at seven o'clock, followed by dinner and "entertainment" in the dining room. More information would be revealed as necessary. There was one rule. We must stay in character and costume for the entire weekend.

With a couple of hours to kill before meeting my fellow sleuths, I decided to immerse myself in my character.

With a gin and tonic from the minibar, I wandered into the en suite bathroom. A roll-top bath dominated the ornately tiled room. I drew a deep, steaming bath, adding a splash of one of the luxury oils provided by the hotel. The aroma rising with the steam was exquisite.

Clipping my hair into a knot, I kicked off my shoes and unzipped my dress, letting it fall to the floor. I abandoned my underwear to the same messy pile and stepped into the tub. The water enveloped my body in a warm, fluid caress that reached my breasts. My dark nipples poked clear of the surface.

I sipped the drink, feeling the gin trace a warm path down my throat. The alcohol and the warm water relaxed me completely.

Using a large sponge, I started to soap myself along the length of my arms, up over my shoulders and across my breasts. As the sponge slid over my nipples, they started to tingle and I concentrated my soaping there, rubbing the sponge round and around. Each time it brushed my nipples, a shiver radiated down my stomach and between my legs. I moved the sponge faster, building up a delicious friction while my free hand stroked down my belly, over my shaved mound, to slip between my thighs. I buried my hand deeper, raising my knees and resting them against the sides of the bath.

I sought my pussy, tracing the fleshy folds surrounding my tight opening. Parting the folds, I slipped a finger inside me, slowly circling to find my G-spot. I rubbed, feeling the tension rise, and within moments I could feel myself edging closer and closer to coming. But wanting to savor it for a little longer, I slowed down my fingering and let my juice-coated finger slip from me.

I started to glide my fingers along the length of my slit, creeping closer to my clit with each stroke, knowing the moment I reached it I would come. Finally, I allowed myself to reach the nub of swollen flesh between my legs. I stroked and pinched it, gasping until my orgasm jolted through my body like a bolt of electricity. I thrashed about, creating a tidal wave of bathwater that spilled over the roll top and onto the floor. Shuddering, I drew back my hand and lay in the water, letting my breathing and heart rate slow down while enjoying the feeling of warmth spreading from my sex.

After recovering, I stepped from the bath and patted myself dry with big, soft towels, dropping them to the floor afterward to soak up some of the splashed water.

I walked naked into the bedroom, my body aglow from its recent exertions. I smoothed a heavily scented body lotion over my limbs and torso, adding a spritz of perfume between my breasts. I reapplied my makeup and at last it was time for me, Lisa Carter, to become Coco for the weekend.

I pulled on a pair of black French knickers, the smooth silk molding itself to my curves. I added a matching bra, suspenders and seamed stockings, taking my time to ensure that the seams running the length of my legs lay straight. I looked in the mirror, happy with my reflection. For the first evening I had chosen an emerald-green, vintage evening gown epitomizing my glamorous character. A pearl necklace and earrings, black Mary Janes and a beaded evening bag completed the look. I unclipped my hair, letting my dark curls fall onto my shoulders. A final slick of red lipstick and Coco was ready to face the world.

On entering the bar, I accepted a glass of champagne from a waitress carrying a large silver tray of flutes. I reveled in the lustful looks I was getting from the men and the envious glances of the women in the room. It boosted my confidence and I knew I would enjoy myself. The men were wearing dinner suits and the women were in evening gowns. It was truly a glamorous affair.

For the next half hour I (Coco?) mingled with the others. I flirted with the men, touching their arms when we spoke, my gaze lingering a little longer than was necessary, and swaying my hips whenever I walked, knowing full well how the dress hugged my body. I embraced Coco with vigor. I loved being her. And everyone else embraced his or her character, too. I couldn't tell who was a guest and who was an actor, everyone played his part so well.

Soon a footman ushered us into the dining room, where we took our places at an elaborately set dining table. The silverware gleamed, the crystal sparkled and huge candelabra bathed the room in a flickering mantle of light.

The general chatter was continuing through the first course when a scream brought the conversation to an abrupt halt. The waitress who had served the champagne ran into the room sobbing, "He's dead, he's dead," again and again. A distinguished-looking gentleman, introducing himself as Sir George Montague, rose from the table. He hurried over to the distressed waitress, ordering her to show him what had happened. We followed them into the adjacent billiard room, where a man lay facedown on the floor, a knife protruding from his bloodstained back. Things were getting exciting.

Sir George took charge, ushering everyone back to the dining room and requesting that a waiter call the police. He encouraged us to enjoy our meal while we awaited their arrival. The conversation had stepped up a notch now. One or two people dropped nuggets of information into the chatter. The dead man, Frederick Deville, who had earlier enjoyed champagne in the bar with the rest of us, had been seen leaving the bedroom of a prominent and married lady. Another guest complained that she had had some jewelry stolen and had seen Frederick in the vicinity of her room. Gradually, a picture of the victim began to emerge, along with a number of motives for his slaying.

As the last spoonful of Belgian chocolate torte slipped down my throat, the doors to the dining room burst open and two men strode in. The first was tall, powerfully built, with an authoritative air. The second man was also tall but slighter, with dark eyes that immediately scanned the room, noticing everyone present.

The first man moved to the head of the table, commanding everyone's attention. "Good evening," he said, his voice as strong as his body. "I am Inspector Harry Winchester. And this man," he waved a hand toward his colleague, "is Sergeant Price. We are investigating the murder of Frederick Deville, the unfortunate chap found dead in the billiard room." He paused and looked around the table. "Sergeant Price and myself will be talking to each of you to try and establish who killed Mr. Deville. I must warn you that you're all under suspicion and it's in your own interests to assist in unmasking the murderer. I assure you that by tomorrow evening at the latest I will have made an arrest and one of you will be facing trial and the hangman's noose."

A middle-aged woman turned to me and whispered, "He's very good, isn't he? I wouldn't mind being interrogated by him."

I smiled and replied, "Who knows, you may get your chance." She giggled and raised her glass.

The two policemen split up to interview us in turn. Meanwhile we formed little groups to discuss the murder. Over the next couple of hours theories abounded, accusations were made and tears and tantrums occurred. Sergeant Price quizzed me for a while. His questions were clever and I realized that the game had started the moment we arrived at the hotel. He asked about people I had seen, what they had been doing, and suddenly, I was suspicious of my fellow diners. Was the lady I passed in the corridor really waiting for her husband? Was the man who stepped outside only in need of a cigarette? Innocuous events took on sinister meanings. I was having a good time, though, almost believing I had stepped back in time and my real name was Coco. I'm sure I wouldn't have replied if anyone had called me by my real name.

The evening flew by and Inspector Winchester announced that he would continue his investigation the following day and no one was to leave the hotel. We all wished each other good night like we had known each other for years and the room emptied as, one by one, we headed to our rooms.

I had reached the staircase when a firm hand took hold of my arm. I spun around and looked up into the face of Inspector Winchester.

"I don't think I've had the chance to ask you any questions yet, Miss," he said.

"Well, I was about to retire for the night. Maybe your questions can wait until the morning?" I replied.

"I don't think so. I'll come with you. We'll talk in your room."

"I hardly think that's appropriate. I have my reputation to think about."

"A man's been murdered tonight. Your reputation is not high on my list of priorities." He tightened his grip and started to mount the stairs. I had no choice but to go with him. As we made our way, a tremor of excitement worked its way along my spine and I was conscious of his hand gripping my arm.

When we entered my room, he let go of my arm and I walked over to the minibar. "I'm having a gin and tonic," I said. "Can I tempt you?"

"A whisky would be good."

"Even though you're on duty? Shame on you." I poured the drinks and handed one to the inspector. He drank it in one gulp.

"So can you tell me where you were before dinner?" he asked.

"I was in my room the whole time from arriving until I went down for dinner."

"Can anyone confirm that?"

"No, I was alone." My heart rate quickened as I sensed we were playing a dangerous game. "I took a bath and spent my time preparing for the evening."

The inspector walked around the room. He opened the bathroom door, observing the wet towels on the floor. He also noticed the puddle of water that the towels had failed to fully absorb. "It seems as though there was an awful lot of splashing for just one person." He turned to face me and I felt the heat rise in my face at the memory of my bath time.

He closed the door and continued around the room, opening and closing drawers as he went. He pulled a red velvet bag from the third drawer he opened. "What's this?" He held the bag toward me.

"Nothing," I gasped. By now the blood had pumped to my

face and I could feel myself burning. I could only squirm with embarrassment as Harry spilled its contents onto the bed. A large, beautifully crafted glass dildo slid out along with a bottle of lube. I had not been expecting company this weekend.

Harry picked up the dildo and held it toward me. "Is this some kind of weapon?" he demanded.

My throat dried up. "No," I whispered. "It's a toy." I had never felt so embarrassed in my life but I was getting incredibly turned on at the same time. I could feel the silk of my panties getting damper by the minute. There was excitement in this man's almost aggressive questioning.

"A toy? It looks threatening to me. Let's put it away for now." He walked to the fridge of the minibar and placed it inside. "I think you're hiding something from me." Harry took off his jacket and placed it over the back of a chair. He sat down and leaned back, crossing an ankle over his knee. "I should search you for any weapons."

"I don't have any, honestly."

"Take off your dress."

I knew I shouldn't but I yearned to do exactly what he told me. I felt a thrill in being ordered about by this man, so I unfastened my dress and let it slip to the floor. I stood before him wearing only my underwear. I was conscious of Harry's stare as he looked me up and down, so I pushed my shoulders back in defiance, which thrust my breasts forward. The lace cups of my bra barely covered my nipples. "See? I have nothing to hide."

Harry licked his lips. "Now your bra."

I felt a wetness between my legs as I obeyed him and reached behind to unclasp my bra. I slid the straps down my arms, holding the cups against my breasts for a moment before letting it fall to the floor. I nodded toward the bulge growing in the crotch of his trousers. "I think you're the one concealing a weapon."

Harry pushed himself up from the chair and stepped closer. "Shut up. Take off your panties."

"I really don't thi—"

"Now!"

I hooked my fingers into the sides of my panties and did as I was told. I faced him dressed only in my suspender belt, stockings and Mary Janes.

The inspector walked over and grasped my breasts in his large hands and I heard a groan escape his lips. He leaned forward and placed his mouth, still warm from the whisky, over a nipple. He started flicking it with his tongue, nibbling and sucking, all the while squeezing and stroking my other breast.

I was so wet I could feel it dribbling down my thighs. I put my hands on either side of Harry's head and raised it until our lips met. His kiss was hard and hungry, his tongue invading my mouth. He pressed himself close and his cock pushed against my naked stomach, only his clothing separating us. I reached down, unbuckled his belt and unfastened his trousers. He kicked off his shoes and his pants quickly followed. He stood there wearing just his shirt, tie and boxers, which were stretched to capacity. I reached inside and took hold of him. He was huge, the biggest I'd ever encountered. My fingers didn't come close to meeting around his shaft.

Harry drew back from me and removed the remainder of his clothes. He threw them across the room and stood naked before me. He was an imposing figure, broad-shouldered, with a strong, muscular chest with just the right amount of hair, but what really caught my attention was his thick cock jutting out from a thatch of dark hair. I started to remove my stockings.

"No," he growled. "Leave them. I like them." He pushed me backward until the bed met the back of my legs and I sat down. Harry pushed me down farther and, taking hold behind my knees, he lifted my legs, spreading them to expose my smooth pussy.

My swollen labia parted and I felt a beating as my heart pumped blood toward my sex. More juice trickled down my thighs. Harry knelt on the floor, gazing at what had been revealed to him, my folds opening to display my secret center. He leaned in closer until his face was only inches away and I could feel his hot breath against my wet flesh. He pushed my legs even farther apart, then suddenly his tongue was sliding up and down my slit, lapping at my juices and exploring every fold until finally he thrust his tongue inside me as deeply as he could.

I squirmed, grasping the bedcover and twisting it in my hands while he sucked, nibbled and invaded my pussy. Then he sucked my clit and I groaned as his teeth brushed the delicate flesh. I wriggled myself against his face, eager to get as much contact as possible as my second orgasm of the day racked my body.

"You like that?" Harry asked as he pulled away. His lips glistened from me and I loved it when he licked them clean, obviously savoring my taste. Before I had time to reply, he used his fingers to spread my lips farther apart and then slowly he inserted two fingers of his other hand, moving them in and out, in and out, almost lazily. Then he squeezed a third finger inside me and I felt so full and stretched. When I thought it could get no better, he rubbed his thumb against my clit with each stroke. I was about to burst with pleasure again when Harry withdrew his fingers and stood up.

I raised my head to see what he was doing but before I could ask him I caught sight of his thick cock pointing upward. It was too much to resist. I pushed myself up from the bed and dropped to my knees before him. Now it was at eye level and I could see his flawless skin stretched taut and the thick cord of vein running the length of his shaft. I looked up, meeting his dark eyes. He nodded and I leaned forward and ran my tongue up and down him, from his balls, over the ridges of his veins to his swollen, silky glans and back again. As his cock twitched, I licked and kissed my way back to his tip again. My nose filled with his hot scent. Without stopping I reached up between his legs, seeking his balls. I squeezed and rubbed them, listening to him groan in pleasure, loving the way they slipped and moved in my hand.

Harry reached down, cupping my face. I opened my mouth wide and took him in my mouth, sucking and licking. My tongue circled before seeking and probing his tiny opening. He started to move his hips back and forth, filling my mouth, and I tilted my head back to accommodate him deeper.

I let go of his balls and slid my hand farther between his legs, finding his tight ring and slowly circling it with my finger, varying the pressure as I went. When I heard him begin to groan louder, I pushed my finger inside him. His buttocks clenched and he seemed to expand even more inside my mouth. I moved my head backward and forward faster, sucking and flicking my tongue. Suddenly hot fluid filled my mouth and I swallowed to make room for more.

He slipped from my lips and I licked the remaining spunk from the end of his cock, all the time looking up, watching his face. Harry's lips were drawn back as he savored the remains of his orgasm. He looked back down to me and said, "I've not finished with you yet." He took my hands and pulled me to my feet. He kissed away a drop of creamy fluid that was trickling down my chin before pushing me back onto the bed.

I expected him to join me there but he turned and walked across the room. I was confused. Had he not enjoyed it? Had I upset him?

Harry walked toward the fridge and opened the door. He took out the glass dildo and walked back holding the translucent toy before him. I felt myself become wet again with anticipation and I lay back on the bed, bending my knees and letting them fall apart, presenting Harry with the perfect target for his glass weapon.

He knelt between my legs and in one smooth movement slid the dildo deep inside me. I gasped as the icy glass entered and my muscles contracted around it. The sensation was exhilarating as the cold glass met my hot flesh. Harry pumped it hard and fast and I rose to meet him, gasping as the sensation flitted from hot to cold and back again with each thrust. I couldn't believe I was about to come again after just a few moments but the pressure inside me was rising and I was about to explode.

Then I came, squirting juice along the glass shaft in a shuddering orgasm. The well-lubricated glass slipped from me and Harry left it lying on the bed between my legs.

Harry stood up and collected his clothing, dressed and walked to the door. "I've no more questions for you tonight, but don't think of leaving." He closed the door behind him. I fell asleep where I lay.

The following morning, there was another murder. A guest was found poisoned. Millie Fanshaw had worked with Frederick, seducing and robbing wealthy socialites.

I had fun making accusations with everyone else. The policemen were a constant presence, revealing clues, questioning more guests. I was disappointed that the inspector seemed to ignore me after my "interrogation" the previous night, but I had to remember that he was playing a part and couldn't ignore the others despite the special attention I had received.

Soon it was over. Sir George was arrested for both murders. The two victims had targeted his only daughter, leaving her suicidal and Sir George distraught, vowing revenge. The other guests resumed their true identities and were dressed in their usual attire and I was Lisa again. It was a shame. I was fond of Coco.

I handed my key in at the reception desk and said my goodbyes, wishing I could remain a little longer.

Suddenly two arms reached round my waist, stopping me in my tracks. Startled, I turned to see who was there and came face to face with Inspector Winchester. Only now he wasn't the inspector anymore. Gone were the suit, tie and Brylcreemed hair. Now he wore jeans and a sweater. His hair was gelled, making him look younger and sexier.

"Gavin!" I blushed.

"I like seeing you that color," he laughed. "Did you enjoy yourself?"

"It was wonderful."

"Told you so."

"It was fun seeing you at work."

"Do you think we could see more of each other at home?"

There was nothing I wanted more. I nodded. "There's one thing, though."

"What's that?"

"Do you think the inspector wants to question me again?"

Gavin smiled, "Oh, yes. Without a doubt."

SURRENDER WITH A TWIST

Suleikha Snyder

Las Vegas invariably made Anna want to do one of three things: blow all her cash at the blackjack table, check out that male strip show at the Excalibur or hook up with a stranger. She'd only been here a day and she found herself doing a fourth thing: *hiding*.

A well-dressed woman, with teased blonde hair that looked like it belonged in 1985, stepped out from a limo. She was immediately flocked by autograph seekers with cell phone cameras. Anna didn't have to be told who she was. She was already ducking behind a pillar and hoping that the reigning queen of "Nights of Surrender" wouldn't see her. Desiree LeBeau played a massive bitch on TV and didn't really have to stretch her acting muscles to do it. Not that she could stretch that many muscles at all, with all the Botox she'd had. *Ugh.* If Desi saw Anna, she wouldn't *hesitate* to bring up Ty. Worse, she'd bring up *Felicity* and Ty. Being divorced for a year didn't make *that* any easier.

Anna made a run for it, bolting inside and hurrying past the roped-off area where some very efficient-looking Emmy staffers were doing check-ins. It would just figure: she'd flown all the way from New York only to run into someone from one of the three remaining New York soap operas.

She wanted to curse whoever booked her a room at the Las Vegas Hilton the same weekend as the Daytime Emmy Awards...which basically boiled down to cursing *herself*. Since their expense budget was nonexistent and the Hilton was one of the cheapest business-friendly options close to the Strip, she'd instructed her assistant to go with it. Sure, crazy events happened in Vegas hotels all the time—when she was meeting a prospective liquor distributor last year, there had been a *clown* convention—but this *really* was beyond the pale. The Emmys? Oh, *hell*, no.

Anna didn't know what it said about her that the only thing *more* trauma-inducing than Bozo and a hundred of his best buddies was a hotel full of soap actors and people who made their living shoving their hand up a Muppet's butt. Not that she was against daytime programming. Hell, she TiVoed "The View" and "Days of our Lives." She just happened to be morally opposed to any events that meant her ex-husband was slated to be in the same confined space. Why hadn't she checked her calendar and *insisted* this expansion meeting take place one week later?

Because you're desperate, Anna, the tiny voice in the back of her mind that sounded suspiciously like her mother reminded. *Because you want to run into Tyler*, added a voice that was more like her sister's. You'd think that Abby hadn't picked *her* side in the divorce, given how she always carried on about Anna harboring feelings for her ex. Not wanting to spend three thousand dollars removing the PROPERTY OF TYLER ST. CLOUD tattoo on her inner thigh did *not* mean Anna was still in love with the insensitive dolt. It just meant she didn't want a laser surgery technician to see what an idiot she'd been at eighteen. She was clearly still an idiot at twenty-eight.

Anna kept her sunglasses on while she gave the red carpet a wide berth. A few Internet reporters were already scoping out their spots, but they wouldn't know her on sight. As she headed toward the little sushi lounge adjacent to the casino, she *really* hoped nobody else from "Nights of Surrender" materialized. Years of cast Christmas parties and charity baseball games and Emmy bashes meant that she was a familiar face. Nowhere near as familiar as Tyler's, of course.

There was no point in denying it; Ty was gorgeous. Six feet three inches of dark-haired, blue-eyed, Australian hunk. He'd been dreamy at twenty, when they'd both been working behind the bar at a 9th Avenue dive, and at thirty he was a serious contender for *People*'s Sexiest Man Alive. Anna had never gotten out of the bar business, and she still looked like the girl next door: straight black hair, brown eyes and a runner's body. She was no match for the beauties that were going to be strutting around in D&G a couple of hours from now. She'd certainly been no match for Felicity Hawkins, who played Desi's daughter and Tyler's new leading lady. *Ugh*, she thought again. Method acting was highly overrated.

With the red carpet arrivals into the theater imminent, the dark, womb-like lounge was empty. The lone bartender was texting or playing Angry Birds, and when she ordered an apple martini, he looked equal parts relieved and annoyed. Her first drink went down easy, and fast, and Angry Birds Boy slid her a second one on cue. He was about twenty-two, cute and definitely mad at the world. His disposition improved exponentially when she scribbled a 25 percent tip on her credit card slip, and he grinned at her before vanishing through the door to the kitchens. Maybe he was going to check out the action at the Benihana. He certainly didn't seem to care if she robbed his station blind while he was gone.

Anna slouched over her drink and checked her BlackBerry. There was already a message from Jim, the promoter from Scottsdale, saying he was excited about her concept. *Thank god* something about today was actually going right. For a few minutes she drank in peace, listening to the muted jingling of the slot machines out on the floor and the occasional burst of laughter. The lounge was intimate and not all that inviting for anyone looking to party. Still, it was only a matter of time before someone walked in.

Someone did, of course. Someone who felt familiar. *Too* familiar.

"You have *got* to be kidding me." It was a cosmic joke. Out of all the ridiculous places to hang out in the Hilton, he'd picked here? Not the Vince Neil cantina or the steakhouse? She didn't have to watch his progress across the bar. Her spine stiffened even before she felt his breath on the back of her neck. Tyler St. Cloud owned every room he walked into. He'd left his stamp on every inch of their one bedroom co-op…and every inch of her body. Her senses knew he was near even before he said a word. Of course, he *did* have to talk.

"Anna, what are you doing here? Come to see me win?"

She studied the rapidly dwindling green liquid in her glass. "Please. You're not even nominated, you son of a bitch."

He laughed, and it made her turn around despite every bit of intelligence screaming at her to resist. "You're still paying attention. That's encouraging."

He was still six foot three, still dark haired, and still blue-eyed. Not that she'd expected any of those things to change in the four months since she'd last seen him. "I wouldn't encourage you if you were the last man on earth."

He shrugged, spreading his arms out like he was about to start a monologue. "Yet, here you are. Of all the sushi bars in all the world..."

Her fingers tightened around the stem of her martini glass, ready to snap it in two. "Go to hell, Tyler. Don't you have a shindig to get ready for?"

He looked so good in jeans and a white button-down that it really didn't matter if he put on a tux or not. He'd own that carpet and the cameras.

"Not nominated, not presenting," he shrugged. "I could skip it if I wanted to, darlin'. Spend the rest of the night with you, catching up."

"You'd skip the glitz to hang out with me waxing poetic about the way we were? *Right*. Don't feed me a line, Ty." Had his eyes always been so damn blue? She tried to swivel back to her drink, but he stopped her, sliding one leg between her knees.

The damn blue eyes were suddenly black with intensity. "It's not a line, Anna. No one could've written us a scene this fucking perfect. You think I expected to walk in here and see my wife?"

"*Ex*-wife," she reminded. But he was right. It *was* straight out of a "Nights" episode: The hero walks into a random bar and sees his ex, what will he do? Meanwhile, in her wrinkled linen suit and bitterness, she didn't fit. Like she'd stumbled in from a sitcom. That had always been their problem...even when they were just dumb kids trying to make it in New York City...the only place they'd fit had been in bed. *"Ty, you're too big. I can't..." "Yes, you can, baby. You can take it all. Just trust me..."*

Anna had to curse herself again, because the memory flashed into her head in Technicolor and spread across her skin like a hot blush. Tyler, so close—too close—couldn't miss her response. His knee rubbed against her thigh, scrunching up the skirt of her business suit. *Property of Tyler St. Cloud.*

"Go away, Ty. I have plans," she forced herself to say, fully aware that her body was saying something else entirely.

"Let me guess: blowing all your money, seeing Thunder From Down Under and fucking a stranger?" His eyebrows drew together, arrogant and adorable at once. "Has that *ever* worked out for you?"

"There's a first time for everything," she snapped.

"I know. We experienced most of them together." Ty knew exactly what to say. Exactly how to touch her. His fingers were under the hem of her skirt now, stroking her inner thigh… skating all the way up to where the cursive script declared she was his. She wanted to shove him. No, she wanted to yank him closer. He ducked his head and whispered hot and low against her ear. "Rewrite your plans, Anna. Blow *me*, let *me* strip for you…let *me* be your stranger."

It sounded like a bum deal…except that Ty knew how much she'd loved sucking him off. She'd gone to her knees for him in clubs, airplane bathrooms, at the last Emmys in New York and the one after that in L.A. She'd loved knowing he was helpless to do anything but pull at her hair and beg her to let him come. Sometimes it was all it took to get *her* off, too. Her breath came out in a ragged shot. "Y-you're a stranger all right, Tyler. I don't know you at all."

He grasped her face in his free hand while his other continued its seductive journey. "That's horseshit. You've always known me. You're the only one who's really known me," he swore. "You've gotta believe me. Felicity was a mistake."

"So is this." But instead of pushing him away, she leaned into him, bracing her hands on his shoulders as he worked his hand past the elastic of her panties. "You're going to end up blind itemed: 'What daytime hunk was canoodling in public?'"

"Fuck 'em. I don't care, Anna," he growled. He'd been in the States a long time, but when he was frustrated his accent came out thick. "Anner," he called her now, sinking knuckle-deep into her wet heat. "They can all bloody watch me."

As if Ty had willed it into being, the punk kid bartender reappeared from the back...and promptly stalled in his tracks, all big-eyed and stunned. Anna knew she should say something, make Ty stop, but this felt too good. It felt too right. The bar was chest high. Surely it hid exactly what Ty was doing to her. Leaving her face, her muted moans, and Ty's victorious "Fuck yeah" as the only giveaway.

We can't do this, she thought. *We shouldn't*. But another part of her was thinking that if Angry Birds Boy didn't like the floorshow, he could call hotel security. They could kick her out, and her whole problem of being stuck in a confined space with soap stars would be solved. Making her remaining problem *this*. Her ex-husband's hand between her legs, his gorgeous blue eyes daring her to resist him.

"Ty...this is crazy. *You're* crazy."

"The show put us up at the Wynn. It's either here or your suite, Anna."

Here, cried a voice that wasn't her mother and wasn't Abby. It was the voice that only belonged in her bedroom, saying things like "please" and "yes" and "harder." Anna gave into it just long enough to come. Just long enough to ride Ty's palm and muffle her gasps against his throat. He tasted like salt and oranges. Like a reckless Sunday afternoon in a hotel lounge with an audience of one. She was still shaking, still catching her breath, as Ty swung her off the bar stool and grabbed her purse. "Upstairs," she whispered, blushing as she caught the bartender's gaze over his shoulder. "Let's go upstairs."

During the ride up to Anna's suite, stuck in the elevator with a couple of tourists fresh from the pool and a few writers from "General Hospital," it was all Tyler could do to keep from touching her again. He could smell her on his skin, still taste her, and he wanted to shove her against the wall, hike up her prim little skirt and show everybody who she belonged to. Who she'd *always* belonged to.

Anna. Here, of all places. Tyler couldn't wrap his brain around it. Christ, it was unbelievable, but here she was standing beside him, pretending to watch the floors go by. She looked amazing. Like she hadn't aged a day since he first met her. Like it hadn't been months since the last time he saw her. And not five minutes ago, he'd gotten her off with some stupid voyeuristic kid watching. She was so ready, so open, and they hadn't even kissed yet. He knew her mouth would still be spectacular. Soft and smart and spicy. No screen kisses had ever stood up to the way she gave him her tongue. She'd given him everything, and he'd wasted it. But Ty wasn't going to waste a single moment now.

Award show be damned. He hadn't wanted to fly out to Vegas with Desi, Felicity and the others. He preferred spending his Sundays watching rugby, to be honest. But now, with Anna so close, brushing up against his side every so often, the twentieth floor of the Hilton couldn't come soon enough. Neither could he. When the doors opened, he practically carried her out of the lift and down the hall.

"Ty, for god's sake, you can put me down. I know how to walk." She elbowed him in the ribs, too, but that was the sum total of her resistance. She melted into him like butter, her hair wrapping around his neck and her leg rubbing against his. Her voice was husky with need, and if he had to place bets—which he very well could, given that there was a casino downstairs—he'd say she hadn't been with anyone else since him. How could she, when his name was still etched on her skin?

Anna had always been the strong one, the independent one, knowing what she wanted from her career from the very beginning. When he'd still been answering every casting call his agent sent his way, she'd been putting together a business plan for the bar she wanted to open. She was so in charge. But in bed with him, she'd happily handed him the keys and let him drive.

Tonight, *she* had the key. And they were barely over the threshold with the door locked safely behind them when she murmured, "Okay, Ty. *Strip*."

No muss, no fuss. She'd been promised a little thunder from his down under and she wanted it now. She hadn't changed a bit. Laughter exploded out of him like a cannonball. "What, you're not even going to pay the admission price? I'm hurt."

"Isn't that what I did downstairs?" Her perfect black eyebrows arched up in amusement. He wanted to lick them. To lick *all* of her. "Or do you want me to shell out for the two-drink minimum, too?" She glanced down, making it absolutely clear what she would knock back a shot of.

He was already hard, but that just made him harder, until he was chafing against his boxer briefs, feeling every ridge on his zipper fly. He couldn't have scripted this moment any better. Anna, who got him hard with a look, with a promise, was the best scene partner he'd ever had. He just had to show her.

He started with his shirt burtons, going slow as he backed her farther into the room. She urged him on, his own personal director. Her big, brown eyes telling him just how slow to go, her sighs telling him she liked it when he touched himself.

He was the one who'd gotten her all obsessed with that idiotic Australian strip show at the Excalibur. He was just egotistical enough to think that the only reason she wanted to see a bunch of boys from Brisbane parade around in leather was because she missed him.

"I didn't," she murmured when he said it aloud. "I didn't miss you at all, and when I realized the goddamn Emmys were here, it was the last place I wanted to be." But she was rubbing her throat, fiddling with her jacket like it was itchy. When she shrugged it off and it joined his shirt on the floor, he knew she was lying.

"I think you *hoped* you would see me, Anna." Tyler moved toward her, unbuttoning his jeans and undoing the fly. "I think you knew exactly what you'd find when you got here. Who books a room at the Hilton when you could have the Bellagio or the Mirage?"

She made a face—a scowling, frowning, beautiful face. "That's funny. I feel like I'm seeing a mirage right now. It looks like the boy I married." Then she reached for him, hooking one hand around the back of his neck and tugging him to her. *Finally*, said a voice in the back of his mind as she kissed him. It was fierce, sloppy and abso-fucking-lutely perfect. She tasted like apples, cheap vodka and the girl who'd given him one wild weekend in Rio when he turned twenty-five.

She pulled back just long enough to breathe, to trail words along his jaw with damp, fruity lips. "You really missed me? You really missed this?" There was still that hint of disbelief in her voice, and he couldn't blame her. All he could do was try to drown it out, slanting his lips against hers.

She slid her hand into the undone V of his jeans, diving into his briefs and stroking him like he'd stroked her in the bar.

"Christ, Anna," he swore into her mouth. "Way to take things in hand." He didn't have her name tattooed along his groin, but he was her property just the same. He helped her shuck his jeans and briefs and when he was throbbing, slick with precome, against her palm, she all but confirmed it. She cupped him, barely even squeezing his cock, and he practically spilled right then. Like a boy with his first hard-on. He laughed, raggedly, leaning into her. "Darlin', if you're looking for that blow job I promised…I don't think I'm going to last."

Her eyes were wide open, dark and pure like the absolute center of a flame. Her hand fisted him up and down in slow, torturous strokes. "You were never one for keeping your promises, Ty. That was always my territory."

Tyler accepted it like a choreographed slap, as his due. Then he walked her backward toward the bed, falling down with her and pressing naked skin to clothed. His cock was aching, begging for release, but he struggled—fought, *won*—to ignore it as he tugged her skirt up around her hips and tore at her staid, white blouse. "Then keep the biggest one: to have me and to hold me, from this day forward."

She spread her knees for him, rising up just slightly so he could slide her panties down her legs. "Like I said before, Ty. Not if you were the last man on earth." Her words were clipped, closed, cynical, but the rest of her was flushed, soft and honeyed…

Property of Tyler St. Cloud. "Anna, when it comes to you, I *am* the last man on earth." He set his tongue to the swirling letters, tracing each one, lingering until she was moving restlessly beneath him. Only when she gasped out, "Ty, *please*," did he crawl back up and settle between her legs. He was painfully hard, ready to bury himself deep inside her. Ready, except… "Dammit, Anna. I don't have anything with me. Are you safe?"

"Does it matter?" Her fingers were in his hair now, clutching him tight. "If you're going to leave again...I might as well have a part of you, right? Something to remember you by besides alimony?"

For someone who was a consummate planner, who'd kept him buying condoms for nine years, that was the most ridiculous logic. He was 90 percent certain she was being sarcastic. But Ty couldn't care. Not when he was so close and she was so close and...*and she would look so damn gorgeous carrying his baby*, added the breathless, horny voice from the addled part of his brain. "I won't leave you. Not ever again. Definitely *not* if you have my kid." It wasn't the sexiest of declarations, not something any writer would win an Emmy for, but Tyler meant it. And he meant it when he thrust into her in one, smooth movement. "Property of Anna Chan St. Cloud," he whispered as he sank in to the hilt. "Do you hear me?"

She took him like a glove, sheathing him in wet silk. "I've never needed to hear you, Tyler. I *feel* you. I always feel you."

Something snapped within them at the same time. He grasped her hips, pounding into her like fucking her was the equivalent to breathing. She met him, matched him and echoed him with her kisses, tongue moving against his, licking the inside of his mouth. Her feet beat a rhythm against his lower back, her nails dug into his shoulders. Ty hadn't earned this, hadn't worked for it, but he couldn't let it go. Not until he was spilling deep inside her and she was following him into sticky, sweaty oblivion. It lasted forever...and not nearly long enough.

It was like coming home—coming home to a house wrecked by storm and hearing nothing but thunder. He was broken, too, by the end of it. Sprawled across her, smiling like an idiot. "Well, Anna. What d'you think? Best Performance by a Lead Actor or what?"

She reached up and palmed his face, touching him with more tenderness than he would ever deserve. "If I wasn't lying down, I'd give it a standing O."

It wasn't forgiveness. It was better. It was a chance.

UNBOUND AT THE HOLIDAY INN

Lily K. Cho

I'm a quiet girl; people think I'm shy. I'm not, but the sarcastic and awesomely witty comments running through my mind usually aren't appropriate for polite conversation or small talk, so I tend to keep them to myself. My Asian features and petite stature conspire with my silence so that I am constantly underestimated or overlooked. This has worked well for me in the past, as I don't really like people anyway, but sometimes I do long to let my inner self out to play.

Most of my adult life has been spent being a supportive wife as my husband chased his career goals and traveled across the country, and being a doting mother as I raised our children. I packed lunches and made dinners and never complained, but I always felt there was something missing from my life, some adventure that was slowly slipping out of reach as I got older.

I came to realize that the ingredient missing from my life was passion. I loved my husband; I loved my kids. I loved my house with the tile entryway and granite kitchen counters. I had a good life. But what was I really passionate about? When was the last time I had felt that fire inside?

Mark and I had a successful marriage. We were friends and partners, and Mark was a good husband, provider and father to our kids. But sometimes we both felt like the spark just wasn't there, preoccupied as we were with the daily routines that were both stifling and comforting. We'd been working on it, though, trying to add a little spice here and there. Now that the kids were a bit older, we'd started leaving them with my mother and taking the occasional weekend trips to Napa Valley, indulging in a bit of romance and luxury at a lovely old Victorian hotel. The rosewood furniture and antique decor were quite charming, and after a nice meal at a quaint restaurant, we'd take a bottle of California wine back to our suite and make love for hours. He'd lay me back on the soft Egyptian cotton sheets and pleasure me gently and patiently with his tongue until I'd climax with a soft whimper, then he'd climb on top and take his own pleasure.

I'd surprised him on his birthday a few months back with some naughty little toys. Blushing furiously in the privacy of our hotel suite, I'd presented him with two packages. The first was a vibrator, a pink jelly rabbit model, which wasn't so shocking, after all, as the motor had finally burned out on Old Faithful a while ago. It was the second item that made his jaw drop in surprise, and I think he was blushing, too. It was a bondage set, all black nylon straps, Velcro, and shiny metal hooks like the ones on dog leashes. It even came with a blindfold.

That was a night to remember, as we experimented with the straps, carefully fastening them so they wouldn't scrape the heavy wooden posts of the bed frame. I remember lying on the bed, cold and vulnerable in my nakedness, as he tied me down. First my right wrist, tenderly wrapped and secured in the soft cuff, then my start of surprise as he quickly shortened the tether, pulling my arm toward the corner of the bed. I laughed a little, enjoying the thrill. I'd never been tied down before! My right ankle was next, the Velcro cuff, the sharp tug to remove the slack. Testing, I tried to pull free, but I was caught fast. I could feel my breathing quicken as I realized just how helpless I was going to be, and I was shaking just a bit as my other leg was tied. I must have let out a little whimper, because Mark stopped and asked if I was okay. I nodded, speechless, my mouth dry. I started to panic as he came around to my left arm, my last free limb, and I gave an involuntary jerk as he reached for me. I took a deep breath and reminded myself how much I loved and trusted this man, and lifted my arm so he could slip the cuff around my wrist. My entire body was trembling by then, and I could barely lift my head for him to get the blindfold on me.

He used me well that night, slowly at first, the vibrator playing around my clit before dipping inside, then plunging deeply, relentless, until I came with a cry that surprised us both. He didn't stop, though, instead turning up the vibrations until I thought I couldn't take any more. My clit was so sensitive in that postorgasmic state. I couldn't stop him, couldn't close my thighs, though I tried, couldn't escape the pleasure/pain, though my hips bucked and twisted, and it wasn't until my cries became shrill and frantic that he stopped that delightful torture, freed my legs from their ties, and fucked my quivering pussy mercilessly until he came.

We kept the cuffs for special occasions when we had the time and privacy to indulge. There was something magical about being bound and blindfolded, something that released my inhibitions in a way I had never been able to before. I loved having no choice but to climax at his will, as many times as he'd make me. Still, in the back of my mind, I wondered what it would be like to be the one in charge. I enjoyed being a little submissive, but there was that private part of me that wanted to be in control for once.

When my birthday came around, Mark suggested we go on our typical Napa getaway. It was my fortieth, and he wanted to make it special for me—a weekend of being spoiled, complete with champagne, a chocolate tasting and a spa day for two. He was a little surprised when I declined, knowing how well I liked to be pampered, but I was hungry for something different.

I made the arrangements for my own getaway. Mark wanted to help, but I insisted on doing it myself. I made reservations and packed a special bag for the night. The children were sent off to their grandmother's, and I spent the afternoon alone with a hot bath, soaking in skin-softening oils. My hands drifted down under the surface of the water, fingers slowly making their way to my pussy, playing with the curls there. I had an idea suddenly, and with a wicked grin I reached for the towel and the razor.

I climbed out of the tub and hastily dried myself, then spread a fresh towel on the floor in front of the full-length mirror. I brought a large bowl from the kitchen, filled it with warm water, and placed it carefully on the towel, then arranged scissors, razor and shaving cream nearby. I sat down nude in front of the mirror, legs spread, and really looked at the mound of my sex. I clipped the hair short with the scissors then rubbed some shaving cream over the fuzz. It was cold, but the metal of the razor was more so as I carefully shaved every curve and fold, rinsing with the warm water. The velvety soft texture of the virgin skin and the cool sensation of air caressing my most private parts fascinated me. As I got dressed, the whispery feel of the smooth satin panties both tickled and aroused me.

I called Mark at the office later and told him where to meet me for dinner. Nothing fancy, and nothing heavy; I didn't want to feel fat on my birthday! Afterward, I drove him to the hotel.

"Holiday Inn? Are you serious?" he asked, disbelieving. "You could pick any fancy hotel, and you wanted to stay here? Honey, I wanted your birthday to be someplace special, not some cheap motel!"

"Oh," I said with a soft laugh, "it *will* be special." That seemed to give him something to think about, and he was quietly curious as I checked us in.

The room was basic: utilitarian, clean and comfortable. Perfect. I wasn't going to play pampered princess; the extravagance of our Napa hotel just didn't seem appropriate for tonight. Mark closed the door and reached for me, beginning to kiss me tenderly. I pushed him away, the palm of my hand flat on his chest. "Get undressed," I said. "Now." That earned me a lift of an eyebrow, but he complied. Tonight was definitely not going as he expected.

I watched him as he undressed, his long fingers working the knot of his tie, undoing the buttons on his shirt to reveal the silky hair of his chest and the firm little nipples I so loved to nibble. He tossed the shirt aside and sat on the bed to remove his shiny patent shoes and dress socks. He stood again to unbuckle his belt, a wicked grin on his face, then his slacks were sliding down to the floor, revealing his long, muscled legs. The boxer briefs followed, and he was naked before me, not quite erect and probably wondering why I was still dressed.

"Sit," I commanded, gesturing to the bed. I didn't wait to see if he obeyed but started slowly removing my dress, revealing my red satin bra and matching panties. He smiled as he realized I was wearing thigh-high hose. I've always loved the snug feeling around my thighs, the way they make me intensely aware of my legs, of what is covered, and what is not. I playfully removed my bra, hiding my breasts behind my hands as I turned around to glance coyly over my shoulder at him. I bent over, presenting my ass, and slowly slipped the panties down, revealing the smooth skin beneath.

Naked now except for the hose and my high-heeled black pumps, I turned again to face him, allowing him to see my newly shaven sex. I stood right in front of him, crotch thrust at his face, letting him inspect my handiwork. He gasped in surprise and tried to grab me. I felt his hot tongue on my skin before I pushed him back onto the bed.

I stared down at him, brown eyes meeting blue, and a small smile formed on my lips. I saw his own answering grin before I bent down to kiss him. Our mouths finally met in a slow, lingering kiss, lips tender and softly nibbling, tongues gently probing. His beard was just slightly scratchy against my chin.

"Roll over," I whispered suggestively, and he quickly did. My eyes drank in his broad shoulders, the golden tan of his smooth, warm skin. I sighed happily and ran my finger quickly down his spine, causing him to squirm a bit. Gently, I grasped his arm, lifted it slightly so I could fasten the black Velcro strap snugly around his wrist. His muscles subtly tensed, then relaxed again. I brought his hands together over the small of his back and tightened the second strap around his other wrist. Bound. I leaned over, my long hair brushing his skin, and asked if he was okay. He nodded, speechless, and I smiled and kissed him again.

He jumped as my open hand struck his buttocks. We both laughed a little at my boldness. My palm stung a bit, and I wondered if it hurt him at all. I hoped it did, just a little. Was this making him nervous, wondering if I'd do it again? I let my hand run over the firm roundness of his perfect ass for a moment, then down to tickle his balls, making him jump again. I started to lick my hand, having seen him do that, then thought better of it. Instead I bent over and licked his buttcheeks, getting them good and wet. He twitched a little under my wet tongue, his eyes closing in anticipation. They flew open with the next smack. And the next. Enough; my hand hurt.

I picked up the next item and leaned over him. I saw him eying me, my lips, my naked breasts. He obediently lifted his head as I started to fasten the blindfold on him, but I stopped. "No," I decided. "I want you to watch."

I helped him roll over onto his back. His eyes widened as I straddled his muscular thigh, my hands slowly sliding up my belly to my breasts. I sighed, enjoying my own caresses, enjoying his eyes on me, on my firm brown nipples peeking from between my fingers.

I saw him craning his neck to watch, so I crawled forward and put a pillow behind his head. I teased him, my tits just out of reach of his eager mouth, before resuming my position over his thigh. I settled down, pushing my sex against his leg, and he could feel the moist lips against his skin. His mouth opened just a bit as I slowly started to grind on him, my head back, my hands on their way to my clit. I moaned just a bit, echoed by his own soft whimper. I looked down to see his bright blue eyes watching, following my every movement. I smiled slyly, dipped my finger down into my wet pussy and then brought it to my lips to taste my tangy sweetness. I leaned down to kiss him, my tongue running lightly across his lips, darting into his mouth to share my honey. I wet my finger once again, rubbing the cream over my nipples. I brought my breasts to his mouth once more, but this time I let him suck on them, first one aching nipple, then the other. He took as much as he could into his mouth, enjoying the taste of my arousal.

I moaned with pleasure before pulling away, but I wouldn't deny his hungry mouth. I knelt above his face, and he raised his head, straining to get to me. I let him lick me with just the tip of his hot tongue, and it felt so good. I lowered myself so he could plunge it into me once, twice, then as his tongue started to circle my clit, I pulled once more out of reach. I wasn't sure who I was teasing now.

I knelt over his cock, only semi-erect, but the drops of slickness at the tip gave him away. I used my thumb to spread the precome over the head of his cock, laughing a little at how much there was, then used my tongue to lick the thick, sticky fluid away. I took him into my mouth, and his eyes closed as his head fell back on the pillow. I gently sucked, feeling the blood rushing to engorge his penis. Soon I couldn't contain it in my mouth anymore, so I started moving up and down his swollen shaft.

I got him good and ready before I stopped. I straddled his hips, his cock flat between his belly and my pussy. I ground down, making us both moan. I stared into the endless depths of summer sky in his eyes, lost for a second, caught helpless in my own passion.

I grabbed my vibrator and rubbed it against my clit, rubbing my pussy against his cock. I stood up over him, one hand on the wall above the bed to steady myself, my other hand working the toy in and out of my pussy. He gazed up at me in fascination, watching it disappear into the depths of my sex, listening to the wet sounds it was making.

"Oh, god," I moaned, "Oooooh…" His breathing was almost as fast as mine as he watched, mesmerized, caught in my spell. I bent my knees a bit and positioned myself so he could see everything. My hand worked faster and faster, and I could feel the muscles inside tightening, so tight…so tight…

"Oh, Angie," I heard his awed whisper, "you're so beautiful when you come!" I could hardly hear him over my own moans, but it pushed me over the edge. He started in surprise as the first hot drops hit him, then his mouth opened wide to catch my gush. I slowed, stopped, laughed a little. I could see my creamy white come on his face and chest. I rubbed my hand across my pussy lips and brought it to my mouth, curious to taste it, then lowered myself onto his face so he could eagerly lap it up. I sighed in contentment as his tongue thrust deep into my still-trembling pussy, causing me to squirt once more until his face and my thighs were wet with it.

Finally I got off of him and reached beneath him to undo the straps. He sat up slowly, hair disheveled, rubbing at his wrists a bit. He grabbed me and we kissed deeply, his tongue pushing into my mouth like it had pushed into my sex, plunging, demanding.

He pushed me onto my back and entered me quickly, one fierce thrust to the hilt. I whimpered as my legs tried to close a bit, but he continued to grind almost painfully into my swollen pussy before withdrawing to kneel over me. He waved his erection in my face, using the tip to part my lips. "My turn," he said, a big smile on his face. I smiled back and opened wide for him, taking him in, licking my own juices from his member. I ran my tongue around the swollen head of his cock, my fingers gripping the base. I sucked eagerly at his length, my hands playing with his balls, gripping his ass to pull him in deeper. His moans excited me, and my hips lifted a little beneath him.

"My turn again," I whispered, pushing him onto his back once more. I climbed on top, straddling him. It took a bit of maneuvering to get his thick cock into me, and then I was fucking him, my hips grinding down in circles as he filled me. I couldn't believe how hard he was, huge and solid inside me. I took it slow, feeling every bit of him deep within. His hands gripped my waist, pulling me down even harder, making me whimper. My fingers found my clit and started rubbing frantic circles around it as my breath started to come faster. I felt almost bruised inside, but Mark was the one well used tonight.

His eyes burned into mine and I saw the fire there, the love and the need, and my own eyes started to overflow, burning tears of passion trickling slowly down. I leaned forward and we kissed once more, bodies pressed together, melded into one. With a final thrust he came deep inside me, the walls of my pussy squeezing him, holding him tight. I shuddered as I climaxed with him, breathless in our enduring kiss, writhing with him, riding the ecstasy until the moment was over.

We take turns now, being in control, being on top. I'm more assertive in other areas as well, and I'm thinking about going back to college. Maybe I'll become a writer. Why not?

TRAVELODGE TESS

Justine Elyot

I spot him in Costa, lolling on one of those high stools, flashing his top of the range smartphone for all to see. As my sights home in on him, I tick off items on my mental checklist: handmade shoes, fake tan, splayed crotch in pinstripes. Or, to put it another way: ostentation, vanity, arrogance. Yes, he's the one. He's perfect.

I spend a lot of time in motorway service stations. It's my job, you see. I have to inspect the facilities and report my findings to a consumer organization. This place apparently rejoices in four-star restrooms and an onsite barber shop. But it's the motel I'm interested in today. And how can I rate a motel without testing the bed?

Everywhere I go, I see men like him. I imagine them coming off some production line conveyor belt as hair gel and aftershave rains down from overhead spray nozzles. Their circuits are loaded with business-speak and self-puffery before they are suited and booted and sent out into the world like a biblical plague.

I wasn't too surprised, on drawing within earshot of my target, to hear him spouting some nonsense about baseline figures.

"Are we in agreement, then, mate? Cool. We'll roll it out over the eastern counties then, once all the ducks are in a row. Yeah, I'll catch you tomorrow for a visioning session. Ciao, mate. Bye."

If it weren't for the words spoken, he would have a nice voice, deep and slightly hoarse, probably the product of talking too much and listening too little. He is good-looking despite the over-styling, and he knows it. Coming up behind him, I note giant cufflinks and a whiff of whatever won the latest GQ Grooming Award for Aftershave. I make sure I pass just an inch or so too close to him. My handbag skims the edge of his table and I hear him put the phone down with a faint clatter once my back is presented to his view. Easy, always so easy. Reaching the counter, I jut out a hip in its tight pencil skirt and ask for a cappuccino in my throatiest purr.

While the barista busies herself, I push out my ass and pretend to be reading the price list on the wall. When he puts his coffee cup back on its saucer, it makes a juddery, wobbly sound. Steady your hands, boy, you're going to need them.

For a midweek afternoon, the café is strangely empty, so my table choice—directly next to his—can't fail to be provocative. I set down my cup and reach into my handbag for my phone. When I cross my legs, letting the side split in my skirt reveal the edge of my stocking top, I hear his breathing deepen and quicken.

I dial my home phone number and talk to my answering service.

"Hi, it's me," I say, with a quick glance at him. He is looking at me. "I'm at the services on the M4. Think I might book into the Travelodge." I finger my necklace. He is still looking at me. "It's been a hard day and I need to relax. So I'll see you tomorrow, okay? Yes, the meeting went well. I'll be in the office first thing tomorrow morning with all the news. Bye."

As I press the off button, he clears his throat. I inhale, waiting for it, waiting, here it comes...

"Did you get caught out by those roadworks just past Heston?"

I turn my face to him. He is smiling, a smile that makes him look like Jaws with better dental hygiene. His eyes, above the dazzle, have a hard, hungry gleam.

"Afraid so," I laugh. "I'm so sick of the sight of cones now. I hope I never see another one in my life."

"I hear you."

"You aren't deaf then."

It's exquisite to see the way his brow rumples and his smile fixes itself into a rictus. I didn't mean to do it, but I couldn't resist. But I must overcome this little self-inflicted setback and get him back on track—the track that leads to my motel bed.

"Sorry," I say with an apologetic little smile. "Do you have to travel much?"

"In my line of work..." he starts, and I switch off. I *don't* hear him, until he stops bigging himself up and starts winding things down with a polite, "Yourself?"

"Oh yes, I'm always on the road. I'm in sales, too, but not quite the same product you deal in." Whatever that is. Something to do with telecommunications whatnots, I gathered from the bits of interminable droning I'd processed.

"Oh, really? What line are you in, then? Let me guess. Beauty?" Such gallantry!

I fake a coy glance down at the table and bite my lip.

"I'm not sure I should tell you."

"Oh, go on," he says, stretching out the entreaty seductively. His hand moves along the table, closer to me, his whole body following it into a lean.

"Sexy underwear."

His Adam's apple drops.

"I've a whole suitcase full of samples in my car."

I think he's forgotten to breathe.

"Wow," he says at last. "Cool."

"Would you like to see some?"

"I, uh, I'm not really in the market..."

"No, I don't want to sell them to you."

He licks his lips, looks up at the light fixture for a moment, as if seeking advice from it. When he looks back at me, his pupils are huge and skittering from side to side.

"Are you...serious?"

"Are you in a hurry? Do you need to get back?"

He stares for a moment longer, then shakes his head vigorously.

"No, I...not at all. I can...I'm free for the rest of the day now."

"Good. Because I'm going to take my suitcase full of silky, scanty panties over to the Travelodge and check in with it. Are you coming with us?"

He smiles again, less sharkily, looking more like a schoolboy invited behind the bike sheds for the first time.

"Wow," he says again, then, "Sure."

Long fingers tug at his collar, though his tie doesn't need straightening.

I slide off my stool and extend a hand, which he grabs with indecent haste.

The barista, fascinated, pauses in her drying of crockery, the towel flapping over the counter.

I nod and grin in her direction as I lead my lamb to the car park. If I could, I'd drag him by his tie. The vivid orange silk matches his skin tone, I notice.

Not many people are hand in hand as they mill around the convenience store and the Burger King. Most of the nonstop human tide swelling in and out of this place looks tired and cross, slouching in tracksuits, munching on overpriced junk. Some of them stop and stare at us, the polished pair with our eyes on the motel and our minds on sex. It makes me smile and sway my hips.

I feel all-powerful in the car park, heaving my suitcase out of the trunk. I want sex. I take it.

He wrestles the baggage off me, saying something about my being a "lady," and tries to beat me to the motel, because it seems to be important to him that he gets into the lobby first. He does the alpha strut all the way across the forecourt and makes the booking in his name, which I don't bother to remember. I guess that means he'll pay with his credit card. The lack of wedding ring wasn't just a travelling salesman's ruse. My conscience can be clear.

"Room Two-Sixteen, turn right when you come out of the lift."

The clunky key is given to him, and he wheels the suitcase into the lift, where it stands awkwardly between us, but not so awkwardly that I can't wrap a fist around his tie and yank him down for a clash of lips and teeth the moment the doors slide shut.

He smells like heaven by the motorway, fresh spice and petrol and coffee and spearmint all mixed with pheromones and flesh. He is lean and hard, the way I like them, and his lips don't take prisoners. Neither do mine. We kiss all the way along the corridor, bumping into the walls, bruising our ankles with the suitcase, grabbing handfuls of well-cut cloth as we go.

When we get to the door, he can hardly fit the key in the lock, and then there is a competition over who gets to push whom into the room, which I win by making him trip over a suitcase wheel.

He sprawls on the thinly carpeted floor, swearing, and I shove the suitcase into the cupboard beside the door and lock us in.

"Christ, are you always this feisty?" He is reaching for me, trying to grab a leg to pull himself up. I put my foot on his chest and survey his supine form.

"Oh, yes," I say. "I'll wear you out. I hope you don't mind."

His hands circle my ankle.

"Not at all." His rakish smile doesn't look right from this angle, but it works to distract me while he sets about pulling me down on top of him. "As long as I get to wear you out, too."

"Sold, to the salesman in the sexy suit," I hiss, mussing his floppy hair with my sibilants. I pull at his tie, loosening it, while he rolls me over and takes an extended kiss from me before hauling me to my feet.

Our progress to the bed is like a bad tango, feet everywhere, but when we fall on top of the ancient duvet, the dance takes on an intense choreography. His tie comes off, then my jacket, a kiss, a slap on the seat of my skirt, stretched across my ass, a pinch of his neck, heavy breathing, steam. His jacket clinks when it hits the floor and loose change rolls under the bed but I am on him, my palm flat on his fresh white shirt, taking my fill of the heat of his chest and the savagery of his mouth. His arm clamps me tight and he gets me underneath him, pinioning my legs with his knees, fingers working briskly on my buttons while he pants into my face.

"You're getting it," he informs me. "Hard."

"Harder the better," I say, reaching down to squeeze the bulge at his crotch. "Oh, hello. You meant that, didn't you?"

"I don't say it if I don't mean it, darling."

"Call yourself a salesman?"

But my shirt is off, and he is winning the undressing race. I need to up my game.

"Why the fuck are you wearing a waistcoat?" I complain, snagging a nail in a buttonhole. "How am I supposed to strip you down?"

"Wish I'd known…" he said. "Didn't know I was gonna be… fucking you…"

He silences me with another kiss, his hands all over my bare stomach and ribs and arms, moving toward their goal: my breasts in their sheer-cupped black bra. The waistcoat goes the way of the jacket but I'm buggered if I know what to do with those cufflinks. I focus instead on his belt—heavy leather, my favorite.

My movements are slowing, the drug of lust working its toxins into my blood, fogging my brain. The urgency is still there, but I've reached a tipping point and now I want the sensuality, too. I like the way he feels and the way he tastes. I want to savor it.

The removal of the trousers is slower, almost languid, but he shows no signs of breaking pace, almost tearing the lining of my skirt in his haste to get it off.

"It's okay," I whisper during a brief absence of his tongue from my throat. "There's no rush. We've got all night if you want."

He kneels up between my legs and looks down at my matching knickers and suspenders. His hair, so perfectly in place before, is standing on end and falling over his forehead. Crumpled shirt, boxers and lurid purple socks. I feel something unwelcome—tenderness?

"I'm making a mess of you," I say, squeezing a strong thigh.

"Oh, just you wait." He's trying to sound intimidating but I find it strangely sweet.

"I can't." I pull my bra straps down over my nipples, deliberately roughly, so that I have to bite my lip at the chafing sensation.

Waiting is off the agenda. We wrestle with fabric and elastic, hooks and eyes, snaps and cufflinks, until no barrier is left between us, except the one provided by an additional wrestle with latex. On top of his earlier scent, there is rubber and sweat and melting hair gel and sex. He seems to be made of these things and I can do little else but crush my face into his chest and breathe him in while he works on the condom he keeps hidden inside his handkerchief. Clever boy.

"How much do you want it?" I ask him. "How much do you want to win?"

His fingers drive inside me, finding me wet, finding me ready.

"I want to win. I'm a winner," he says. "You want it, too. Don't deny it."

My body provides the evidence, opening up for his fingers, taking them in. His face is a thing of wonder, his eyes shining with that "Is this really happening?" exhilaration.

But I have to stop humanizing him.

I arch my spine and spread my legs wider, cupping a breast with one hand, sneaking the other beneath his balls.

"Let's touch base."

He stares at me blankly.

"What?"

"I mean, fuck me, soldier. Give me all you've got."

He understands that all right. He launches himself on me, filling me good and deep from the first thrust home. I clench my muscles tight, squeezing him, grabbing his ass and urging him to go faster, harder, digging my nails into his firm flesh.

He gets hold of my arms and twists them away until I am held down; it seems he doesn't take kindly to my attempts to control his angle of penetration.

"I hate men like you," I say as he powers back and forth.

Without breaking his stroke, he grunts, "What?"

"I hate men like you." I try to keep the words clear, but it isn't easy. "I hate you. That's why I want to fuck you."

"What kind of psycho bitch are you?"

He stops for a moment, braced above me on his elbows, screwing up his eyes to avoid the sweat that's running down his forehead.

"Do you care? Does it matter?"

He looks over his shoulder, as if for an assassin, keeping his hands over my wrists.

"I don't understand. What's going on? What's all this about hating me? Why did you invite me back if you hate me?"

"Because it turns me on. Finding myself on a motel bed, stuffed full of some anonymous arrogant bastard's cock really does it for me. I don't expect you to understand."

"Good, because I don't." He sounds offended and I wait for the critical moment to come, the moment where they either up and leave or just shrug and carry on.

"If you know I hate you, and you carry on fucking me, I will come. But you have to know that I hate you."

"That's so fucked up I can't even—"

"I know. So don't try. Just keep going."

"Crazy bitch," he says, and I half close my eyes and sigh.

"That's it. More of that, you dickwad."

Uneasily at first, then with growing confidence, he resumes the in-out.

"So you want fucking so badly you'll do it with any Tom, Dick or Harry?"

"That's right, you creep."

"Dirty slut."

"Sleazy dog."

"You must need it bad."

God, he's good. I feel my tight inner core start its slow unfurling, my self-control given leave of absence by his softly spoken obscenities.

"I do. Otherwise I'd never let a twat like you past first base."

I wrap my thigh around his hip, pulling him in deeper, giving myself up to him.

"But I'm here now, balls deep in you, sweetheart, and there's nothing you can do about it."

It's growing. It's spreading from the base of my stomach, creeping up slowly.

"I want to slap your face so hard."

"You can't slap anything while you're flat on your back full of my cock, darling, can you?"

"Oh, god. I'm so close."

"You need to know who's boss around here, love. And it isn't you. Take it, go on. It's what you wanted."

"Fuck youuuuu." But I am coming now, hard, bucking and twitching beneath him, my vocal curse all caught up in my orgasm. He knows I hate him. He made me come. I have what I want.

He stills for a moment then rides me hard to his own climax, holding me so tightly, he bruises my wrists. I love to watch their faces when they come, so full of bizarre pride and helpless overwhelming, caught up in something bigger than themselves—a concept they all find problematic.

When he falls, face-first, into the pillow, still on top of me, I put a hand on the back of his neck and kiss his hair.

"Thought you hated me," he mumbles.

"I don't hate you."

"My head's fucked. Why are you doing this to me?"

"How can I hate you? I don't even know you."

He turns tired eyes to me. His expression of profound confusion melts my heart.

"Okay. Don't say any more. I give up."

"I hate what you represent. A particular type of man. Self-assured and overconfident, chauvinistic, ambitious, full of tacky charm."

"Thanks."

"I'm not saying that's what you're like. But you look as if you might be."

"So, do you do this often?"

I sigh. "Yeah."

"Like…for fun?"

I'm quiet for a while.

"I wouldn't call it that. It's kind of…my thing. That's all. I go from motel to motel looking for easy prey. There's a lot of it about."

"Well, yeah. No-strings sex. Most men aren't averse."

"I know that. I think that's the problem. I think, deep down, I hate that they aren't averse to it."

"Yeah, if it's revenge on mankind, I don't think you've thought it through. Hot sex in a motel is the kind of revenge most of us could live with." He pauses. "Perhaps it's not the men you hate."

Damn. He's sharp. Most of them have plankton levels of insight.

"What does it matter?"

He leans up on an elbow, frowning. "It matters."

"You think I should make love not war?"

"If you want to put it that way."

"I tried it once."

"Once. Not a scientific sample then. Try it twice."

I put a finger to his lips.

"Sh. You're sweet. Too sweet for me."

"Show me what's in your suitcase and I'll show you how sweet I am, darling."

I laugh out loud. The suitcase isn't full of saucy underwear—I'm not a saleswoman, I'm a secret shopper for a consumer magazine.

Still, I think there might be something in there to interest him, so, for the first time since I took this job on, I go over to the cupboard and haul it out.

BUSINESS EXPENSES

Elizabeth Silver

The birdcage cart wobbled the whole way from the main hotel to the beachside bungalow, pulling left toward its bad wheel just enough to be annoying. It had been a long couple of weeks, and Javier's mood matched the thunderclouds rolling in offshore in a dark and rumbling way that even he recognized as a sign that he needed to relax or risk striking out at the wrong person. But relaxation was a long way off, especially with Marco still out sick and back-to-back conferences killing all of Javier's days off since the month before.

By the time he reached his destination, Javier had managed to curse everyone from the reservations manager, for overbooking for this particular conference just enough that the hotel had to put a few of the "important" people in the luxury bungalows; to the airline for losing the luggage just long enough that he was somehow the only one around to deliver it, even if he'd already clocked out; to whatever guest that had felt it so necessary to pack two enormous suitcases for a four-day business trip in the first place.

When he had taken this job after graduation, Javier had envisioned long, lazy days off on the beach and parties in the penthouse suites when his father was away, but it turned out that being the owner's son made him the one who had to work the hardest to prove himself. He'd been made front desk manager because of his last name, but every day, every crap job he had to do because there was no one else available and it needed doing, it was all part of showing the rest of the staff he kept the position all on his own. Which wasn't strictly true, but at least his lunches weren't coming in burnt to a crisp anymore, so Javier was pretty sure he'd been making progress.

Which was to say, days like this made him wish he didn't have so much to prove. The last ten or so feet of the path were uphill and covered in gravel, and he took one look at the recalcitrant cart and decided there was no way that was happening. Hefting one suitcase in each hand, Javier carried them the rest of the way, glad that the one thing he had made time for had been use of the on-site gym. Damn cases must have pushed every weight and size limit the airline had.

Javier set one of the suitcases down to knock, but wasn't surprised when there was no answer; the conference people were having a mixer of some sort. The ballroom had been buzzing with people when he'd walked by earlier. Using his passkey, Javier let himself in, maneuvering carefully so as to not bang the cases or screw up the walls. He'd just leave the luggage in the bedroom and then go home, take a shower, maybe jerk off to let off some steam.

But when he got in the bedroom, he stopped cold.

Working in the resort, he'd seen a lot of guests naked. It was surprisingly common for them to get locked out when chasing down the housekeeping cart for extra towels, and then there were the skinny-dippers—both in the ocean and the house pool—as well as the occasional conference attendee who had yet to realize that just because there was an open bar did not mean you had to drink until it closed. But this—this was different.

The king-sized bed was in complete disarray, blankets and pillows all over, and in the middle of it all there were two women. One was pale, her auburn hair twisted up to show the creamy length of her neck as she bent to lick between the dark brown thighs of her companion. The one on her back moaned softly, kneading her own breasts slowly as she squirmed under the other one's mouth.

"Fuck me, that's hot." The words escaped Javier's mouth before he realized it, and then it was too late.

The two women froze and turned to look at him, and Javier stood there for a few long seconds wondering if this was the one thing that would get even him fired. Probably.

He cleared his throat and set the suitcases down as gently as he could. "Your luggage," he said, stupidly. "I knocked, but. Um."

The redhead snorted. "Yes, we see." She crawled up to cover her lover's body with her own, never once looking away from Javier as she treated him to a slow once-over that couldn't possibly have missed the semi he was still sporting.

After a long while, Javier realized he was still standing there. "I'll go now," he said, backing away. "Sorry to disturb you."

"Wait."

The other woman rolled the redhead off her and climbed out of the bed, grabbing a resort-issued robe that she didn't bother to belt up. Tall and curvy, with richly dark skin and her hair kept short so nothing got in the way of her high cheekbones and pale green eyes, she reminded Javier of a panther he'd seen on TV once, stalking its prey. And he sure felt like a bunny.

"What's your name?"

He swallowed. No way. There was no way this was happening. She was probably just getting his info so she could file a complaint. "Javier," he said.

"Javier," she said, drawing out the *ah* like a small moan. "Javi?"

"Just...Javier."

She smiled. "Well, Just Javier, I'm Tonya. And that's my boss, Margo." Tonya rested her hand on his chest, one short fingernail playing with the collar of his dress shirt. "You're not dressed like a bellboy."

"I'm not." It was a struggle, but Javier managed to keep his eyes on Tonya's face, instead of the long, smooth expanse of her body, bare between the sides of the robe. "Front desk. My shift was over, so I thought I'd bring your bags out."

"How industrious of you." Margo rolled out of the bed, grabbing a blouse from a nearby chair and pulling it on. She wore small black lace panties that rode low on her hips like indecent little shorts that stood out in sharp contrast to her fair skin. "And yet, you're still here. Don't you have anywhere to be besides perving on the guests, Javier?"

That got him going. He had no business still being there, and his father would have his head if he found out. Javier stumbled backward, stammering. "I'll go. I'm sorry to have...I'll just... Sorry."

Tonya curled long fingers around his tie, reeling him back in. "Well now, wait a second," she said. "I don't mind if you stay. Do you mind if he stays, Margo?"

"Not at all." Margo was opening the French doors to the bungalow's patio, revealing an unobstructed view of the beach. The storm that had been threatening earlier was looking more like a reality about a mile offshore, with faint flickers of lightning throwing the clouds into sharp silhouette. "Especially since he brought my bag with him. You know I like to play."

A warm, salty breeze snaked through the room, ruffling the delicate material of Margo's blouse and lifting the hairs at the nape of Javier's neck. He waited, unsure if this was really happening, or if they were just messing with him; chances were, he'd finally found the one thing that would get him fired, but if not…well, that tiny chance alone was enough reason to stay put and find out.

"I shouldn't have interrupted," he said. His voice was strangled, like it was his neck Tonya still held. "I should just…"

"Stay." The word was whispered against his jaw a breath before Tonya chased it with a kiss. "Don't you want to?"

Slim hands—Margo's—slid around Javier's waist, flirting with his belt buckle. "Tonya likes it when I watch her get fucked," Margo said. "And I've been looking for new playmates for my toys."

"Toys?" Javier stiffened, and not in a good way. "I don't do that bondage stuff. No one's getting tied up, or I'm leaving."

"Pity." Margo didn't sound at all put off, though. "Get him undressed, would you? I'll get the stuff."

Tonya worked quickly, pulling off his tie, opening his shirt, pushing all of Javier's clothes out of the way in what felt like a few seconds. Before he knew it, Javier was landing on the bed, naked, with Tonya beside him. He kissed her, not sure if it was allowed, but when she didn't pull away, he deepened it, tasting her more and more until they were pressed close, his growing erection trapped between them.

Then he felt Margo, warm and nude, against his back. "Tell me, Javier," she said, kissing his shoulder and caressing Tonya's hip, "have you ever been fucked by a girl before?"

The sound Tonya made was somewhere between a coo and a moan, so it had to be good, but Javier shook his head. "I'm pretty sure you lack the equipment to do that."

"Do I?" Tonya held up something. He had to twist to see it properly, and it still took Javier a few seconds to figure out what the straps and silicone were all for, where the small knob in the middle would go even as the back of his mind forced a picture of the long, purple dildo spreading his asscheeks and fucking him. He'd heard about strap-ons before, but it still took a long while to register that he was looking at one, and that Margo meant to use it on him.

It should have frightened him, and it did. A little. But more than anything, it stirred something dark and fascinated inside, in the part where he'd stayed when he'd seen the women on the bed, where he'd stayed each time he'd tried to stammer out an apology and leave. And Javier liked it. He nodded.

"Okay." The word was barely out of his mouth before Tonya squealed happily and rolled them, exposing his back entirely.

"She's not the only one who likes to watch people get fucked, is she?" he asked, looking down at her. Before Tonya could answer, Javier kissed her neck and moved down, licking and nibbling at her smooth skin. He could hear Margo behind them, heard the clink of tiny belts being fastened around Margo's slim hips and thighs, the familiar click of a lube bottle being opened. Javier tensed, waiting for the first intrusion.

When it didn't come, he relaxed enough to keep kissing downward, tongue sweeping a lazy circle around one of Tonya's nipples before pulling it into his mouth to suck. She arched under him, a lazy push into his touch for more, and Javier sucked harder, scraping her areola with his teeth as he let go, moving farther and farther down.

Her pussy was bald. Somehow, Javier had managed to miss that earlier when he was trying so hard to look her in the eye and not do anything else that might get him fired. Not that it mattered now, as he dipped to taste her navel, teasing her one last time before sinking between her spread thighs, kissing them gently and working his way up to her lips. He opened her up with the fingers of one hand, lightly caressing her inner folds with his index finger.

"Gorgeous," he whispered, and she squirmed under his stare.

"Take a picture, it lasts longer," Tonya said, slinging one of her smooth legs over his shoulder and pulling him in closer. "Come on; lick me. Do it."

Instead, Javier touched her, avoiding her already swollen clit. They must have been going at it for a while before he'd walked in, as wet and ready as Tonya was already, and Javier wondered how much she'd be willing to take before he had to get down to business. He kissed her, just above the cleft of her lips, and circled his fingers around her wet entrance, pushing just enough to make her lift her hips for more, but not nearly enough to breach her. This sort of thing never happened, not ever, and there was no way Javier was going to waste a second of it.

Thunder rolled in the distance, the storm starting offshore. Javier's skin prickled as the breeze turned cool, laced with the sharp tang of ozone, but then he was smoothed by hot, confident hands as Margo touched him, slithering down his body while he licked and touched and kissed closer and closer to his goal, making Tonya gasp a little louder with each try.

Sharp teeth bit into his side, his hip, his ass, marking him as theirs for the evening, encouraging Javier to arch back for more. Tonya's fingers curled in his hair, tugging to keep him in place, and he gave in, sucking her clit into his mouth just as he felt the cold drip of lube over his ass. He couldn't flinch away without losing hair, couldn't take a second to remember how to breathe as a long, slender finger pushed into him, and it was fucking perfect. All Javier could do was moan against Tonya's clit, circling it and flicking it and sucking it while her lover finger-fucked his ass.

One finger, and then two, and he was full, almost uncomfortably full, but Javier kept eating at Tonya, making her cry out as he returned the favor and slid his fingers into her, crooking them to find her G-spot. He wasn't sure he liked what Margo was doing to him, but the distraction of driving Tonya out of her mind was more than enough to keep him hard and ready. Margo pulled out and pushed her fingers back in, more this time, three maybe, and suddenly he wasn't so sure about being ready after all.

But then she twisted her hand and did something, pushed somewhere, and every nerve in Javier's body started singing. It was like the seconds before an orgasm, only it kept on going, on and on, and he was pretty sure she was trying to kill him, but fuck, what a way to go.

By the time Margo pulled her fingers free, Javier had his head on Tonya's hip as he knelt there, panting desperately. His cock hung hard and heavy and ready to blow, and Tonya was petting his hair, laughing softly.

"I think he's good to go, Margo."

"You think?" Javier didn't even mind the mocking laughter in her voice. If the other thing she was planning on doing to him felt half as good as that, then he was signed up and on board, ready to leave port. "Assume the position, Javier, and we can move on to the really good stuff."

He didn't even bother to hesitate; as quickly as he could, Javier was on his hands and knees over Tonya, kissing her slowly as he felt Margo shuffling into place behind him. His stomach clenched as some last-minute fear finally piped up, but he ignored it, widening his stance when she told him to, and trying to relax when the wide silicone head of Margo's strap-on pushed against his ass.

He still tensed and it still hurt, but Margo was slower and more patient than Javier would have expected, rubbing his back and working with Tonya to keep him calm. Finally, he felt the smooth harness pressed against his ass, and knew it was as deep as it could be. He felt full, stretched too thin and on the verge of something he didn't understand. It scared the hell out of him, but like anything else that scared him, Javier embraced it.

"Fuck," he said, panting, head hanging as limp as his dick. "I don't...that's..."

"There's more." Margo draped over his back, pressing her firm breasts against him as she reached for Tonya. "Toni, take it. You know what to do."

She pressed a small black box into Tonya's hand, and then reached under Javier, stroking his flaccid cock. Before he could do much more than think that Margo seemed awfully sure of what to do, Tonya pushed one of the buttons on the box, and the dildo deep inside of Javier's ass began to hum. Margo cried out the same time as Javier, arching behind him and pushing just a little deeper. The vibrations massaged that hot button—his prostate, Javier's brain finally supplied—sending pleasurable shocks up his spine that made Javier entirely forget that he wasn't enjoying this.

"Please," he said, barely managing the single word as his cock filled once more and higher functions became less and less a priority. Margo was moving behind him in tiny little thrusts, her hands gripping his hips like she needed an anchor as badly as he did.

"Please, what?" Tonya asked. She pressed another button and the vibe stopped. "What do you want?"

Javier gulped for air. And then said, "More." He'd wanted

the reprieve—until he got it. It didn't matter now, since all he could think was, "More. Please."

"Dirty boy." Margo laughed, her thrusts lengthening, getting surer. "Get the condom on our dirty boy, Tonya."

With a flick of her fingers, Tonya turned the vibrator back on before rolling the condom down Javier's cock. The combined sensations had him clenching his fists in the bedding, trying to hold on with all his might as it threatened to overwhelm him right from the start. And then Tonya was sliding into position under him, her long, dark legs spread wide and inviting as she guided him into her body.

He tried to go slow, tried to drag out the moment, but then Margo thrust hard behind him, shoving Javier deep into Tonya in one go. A crash of lightning lit up the room, its answering thunder almost drowning out their simultaneous cries of pleasure, and Javier gave up to Margo. He let her drive the pace of the fucking, her thrusts pushing him forward. All he could do was kneel there and take it for long seconds, fucking and being fucked by two of the most gorgeous women to ever touch him.

Then he reached out and covered Tonya's hand, turning up the vibrations. He was so close, but it still wasn't enough; all he could think was *more*.

Tonya laughed breathlessly and hit the button again, maxing out the speed. Then she reached down between their heaving bodies and started working furiously at her own clit, fingers slipping around Javier's length as he moved in and out, her muscles clenching around him over and over as she pushed herself right along with them. And behind them, Margo screamed out her pleasure, shoving into Javier with increasingly erratic strokes, the vibrating dildo hammering against his prostate, massaging him brutally until he broke, coming so hard it almost hurt when Tonya followed, her pussy spasming around him as she came.

Margo pulled back too fast, and the last brush of sensation drove Javier flat, sprawled across Tonya and reaching almost desperately for the remote to turn it off. Thunder rolled outside, the wind picking up like a cool, wet caress over their sweaty bodies, and Javier looked out across the beach as Margo crawled up Tonya's other side, kissing her slowly.

The clouds hung low over choppy waves, already dissipating from the squall, the remains moving farther out to sea. There were no boats on the water, just three buoys to mark the resort's boundaries, dancing erratically in the wind and surf. Javier knew exactly how they felt. He turned back to the two women beside him, curled around each other and still kissing.

"A strap-on, Margo?" he asked. "Really?"

Margo laughed. "Well, you're the one who decided to be a vanilla bellhop. What kind of kinky role-play vacation is this supposed to be if no one gets tied down?"

"Hey, you're the one that wanted to do it over your conference weekend." Javier rubbed his face, trying to get the energy to stand again. "Unless you want to walk around with rope burns?"

Tonya shook her head. "You should count yourself lucky, Javi," she said. "That's not even close to the wildest thing she packed. I should know; I peeked before we left."

"Those lucky security agents at airport screening must've got an eyeful." Javier shook his head and rolled to the edge of the bed, tossing the condom. He needed a nap before another round and a shower before that.

"I always pack my toys with a note, just in case." Margo followed him into the bathroom, and leaned against the door frame. Her long, pale legs were tempting, smooth and slender and almost enough to make him sink back down to his knees and save the shower for later. But that could wait, and Tonya would gladly keep Margo warm while he cleaned up.

"What does the note say?"

"*Please put everything back when you're done!*" Tonya called from the bedroom, laughing.

Margo grinned. "It's funny, though. I think I'm missing a bottle of my best lube. Do you think I can write that off on my expense report?"

RETURN TO THE NONCHALANT INN

Erobintica

Nearly twenty years had passed since they'd climbed these stairs together. Though Gerald and Jillian had visited the island many times over the years since, both separately and together, they'd not stayed at this inn since that fateful trip. His beard was now almost white, her long braid was more salt than pepper, and though they both were still in jeans and carrying backpacks like in their younger days, they moved a tad bit slower.

They'd requested the same converted attic room with the east-facing window, so they could watch the sunrise from their bed, just like they had all those years ago, when they'd first had company. At the top of the last flight of stairs, Jillian turned the key in the lock and pushed open the door.

She wasn't sure what she'd been expecting. They knew the room's decor had been changed several times in the intervening years, since they'd become friends with the innkeepers. When they'd stayed here before, it had been filled with antiques left from the previous owners. Such a prim setting for what had turned out to be anything but a prim visit: Painted iron bed with a pastel quilt. Flowery Victorian wallpaper. Milk glass vases filled with fresh-cut flowers sitting on old oak dressers topped with doilies.

Now the wallpaper was gone and the white paint had been stripped away from the beams. There was a skylight over a custom platform bed. Everything in the room—furniture, lamps, framed sketches, hooked rug, turned wood bowls filled with beach stones, handblown glass vase holding a few sprigs of dried grass—was made by local craftspeople. It was all clean and sensual lines with muted, earthy colors.

"It's so different!" Jillian said.

Gerald set his pack down just inside the door next to Jillian's, and watched his wife move about the room. He never tired of watching her, since she always seemed to put her whole body into whatever it was she was doing. He'd fallen in love with her while watching her paint back when they were both grad students. He'd fallen in love with her strong arms, her slender legs, her cute little ass. He'd also fallen in love with her intensity, her joy with every discovery, and possibly most of all, her passion.

"Oh, look! It's one of Tom's rocking chairs!"

Jillian sat down by the window and began rocking.

"Wonder if it's a coincidence that it's in this room? It would certainly be like Tom to arrange to have it here," Gerald said as he placed his hand on the back of the chair and felt the smooth wood. At first, this almost stopped its motion, but Jillian soon compensated with the muscles in her legs, using just a little extra force. She'd never been one to let him stop her.

"Maybe he has a chair in each room. We'll have to ask him at dinner tonight," she said, reaching back and patting his hand. She got up and headed over to the bed, kicked her shoes off and lay down.

"Come here, Gerry," she said, patting the space next to her, "lie down with me." He left the chair and sat on the edge of the bed, undoing his shoes and setting them carefully aside before stretching out next to Jillian.

She knew that even though they'd become fast friends with Tom over the years, the memory of that week still made Gerald feel a twinge of the hurt that he had been so sure was headed his way. Introducing something new is never easy, she thought to herself. This weekend was an anniversary of sorts.

They'd come here the first time for a collaborative arts festival week, the island filling up with writers, visual artists, and musicians. They'd picked The Nonchalant Inn as their home base that week because they'd liked the name, and because Jillian's friend Annie was staying there.

Jillian and Annie shared a studio then. Gerald had found Annie quite attractive, with her curly red hair (just like her namesake!) and full breasts, but she had a rather butch girlfriend when they first met, and he was happy with Jillian, since she tended to be quite voracious in bed.

It made him a little nervous when he noticed Annie flirting with his wife, and even more so when his wife flirted back. He had a couple of friends whose wives had left them after they decided they were lesbians. He reassured himself that Jillian liked to fuck him too much for him to worry about that. So he allowed himself to fantasize a bit, even imagining them both with him, though he didn't let on to his wife that he had, at least not until later.

"Remember that first time we were here?" Jillian asked as she started playing with Gerald's shirt buttons.

"Yeah, I do. I remember being shocked that Annie was here with some guy, since I figured guys weren't her type," Gerald said.

"I was a little surprised myself," Jillian said as she slipped her hand into his unbuttoned shirt. "And a bit disappointed even. I'd been hoping I'd have some time in the sack with her as well as with you."

Jillian paused to glance at Gerald's face. Even though they'd talked about all this many times, she still felt nervous when admitting that she'd cheated on him with another woman. Back then he didn't even know she had any serious interest in women. But right now, he obviously was just enjoying her hand wandering his torso.

"When she introduced us to Tom, I felt kinda betrayed." Both of them laughed when Jillian said this. "Yeah, ironic, huh?"

Gerald shifted his weight and began stroking the inside of Jillian's thigh.

"Yeah, I remember you being all cranky and bent out of shape that afternoon," he said as his fingers brushed her crotch and crept up to her zipper. "And you started drinking wine as soon as we got down to the dining room." He chuckled as he pulled the zipper down.

"Sometimes I wonder how our lives would have been different if Tom hadn't been…" Jillian's voice fell away as Gerald's fingers slipped between her legs and started stroking her folds. She didn't easily get wet like she used to, flooding at his touch, but he knew how to coax her to arousal.

"Hadn't been what?" he asked with a gentle smirk in his voice. Jillian had always been this way. So easy to distract with just a simple, well-placed touch.

"Been so obviously interested in me. In us, as it turned out."

"All I knew at first was that I felt terribly threatened."

Gerald said this just as he bent in to kiss Jillian's neck. She tilted her head back a bit to make it easier for him. He was silent a moment as he pressed against that spot where he could feel her pulse with his lips.

"Both he and Annie were so blatant, and you soaked it up," he whispered through her hair, which he'd been unbraiding as he kissed her neck. "I remember being really bothered by the way you just seemed to come alive when they both turned their attention on you."

"It was a bit of a roller coaster. I went from being jealous and hating Tom at the beginning of dinner to wanting to drag him into the bushes and fuck his brains out by the time dessert arrived." Jillian stroked the bulge in her husband's jeans. He groaned and pressed hard against her hand. "And I would have, but..."

As they talked, their hands wandered each other's bodies, in no hurry, pleasuring indirectly through cloth or directly on skin. They each knew the other well.

He knew that her back was exquisitely sensitive, and so when she turned away from him, it wasn't because she didn't want to face him, but rather because it was how she indicated that she wanted to feel his touch tracing her spine. Sometimes all he had to do was place a hand gently on her lower back, just above the roundness of her ass, and she could feel the rush of blood to her vulva, could feel the swelling, the warmth.

She knew that sometimes he wanted his cock touched right away, and others he wanted to be teased a bit, even quite a while, before she touched it. In the "old days," as she put it, she would have guessed at which it was he wanted, sometimes being wrong, though not finding out till much later. But eventually they'd learned (they'd had to) that communication—talking about it—made being sexual with each other easier.

"But?" Gerald gently prodded her to continue. Hard to believe that years ago he would have just let the conversation die, preferring to just get on with the sex. But he'd seen how Jillian had bloomed once his encouragement helped her to express her deepest thoughts and emotions. The payback hadn't been bad either, come to think of it.

"Well, I wasn't sure what was going on. Annie and I had messed around some, and I'd really loved it, though there was no talk of starting up any sort of 'relationship,'" Jillian made air quotes, then returned to Gerald's zipper which she'd been about to slide down. "When I saw her and Tom kissing out in the garden before dinner, I was afraid all my fun was over. Annie had been the one to make a move on me, and I knew that I didn't have the nerve to approach anyone else—any woman, that is. Not then."

"Had you approached a guy before?" Gerald was suddenly very curious. He'd never heard Jillian mention any specific dalliances before Annie. Or if she had years ago, he'd forgotten.

"Well, yes and no. There'd been a few guys I'd flirted with pretty seriously, and one in particular I would have done in a heartbeat, but he never gave me an in. I'm pretty sure he knew what I wanted, but he chose to play dumb. At least that's what I think. So nothing ever came of any of that. Unfortunately."

She followed this with a sly smile as she lowered herself to brush her lips along the edge of his boxers. She remembered the shame she'd felt back then about her desire for something more, and she rested her forehead on Gerald's abdomen. He stroked her hair and leaned a knee against her leg in a small gesture of understanding. When he spoke, she lifted her head.

"I know you sometimes feel bad about all that went on in those days. By the time we came here, I pretty much suspected that something was going on between you and Annie. But I guess that I wasn't as bothered because she's a woman. I know it doesn't really make sense when you think about it. But I'm glad that Annie came on to you when she did. And I'm glad that she brought Tom here that time."

"Really?" Jillian had gotten to her knees and looked down at him while she pulled her shirt over her head.

"Yeah. I think I knew instinctively that if you kept trying to deny that part of yourself, the part that needed more than I was willing, or thought I was willing, to give you, you'd start slowly dying inside. It was even starting to show in your drawings. It sure as hell wasn't easy. I guess I figured that if I allowed you anyone else, you'd end up leaving me. Simple fear of competition."

"Ohhhhh." Jillian lay on top of him and snuggled into his neck. "No need for that! And I've never really compared. Honestly."

They kissed a long time, and she felt his erection, which had flagged a little, come back to life. He reached behind her back to undo her bra and paused.

"Do we have time? I have to get ready for my reading before dinner. What time are we meeting Annie and Tom? And I thought you wanted to walk down to the beach and do some sketching."

"We're gonna be here for four days, I can sketch another time. So that gives us a couple of hours before we have to meet them." Jillian smiled as she reached back and helped Gerald with the hooks. All these years and he still hadn't quite figured them out.

They stopped talking and concentrated on sensations. His beard against the skin of her breast as he sucked at a nipple. Her knee, sharp and hard as she pressed up against his scrotum with it. At one point they both got up and turned back the covers on the bed and took their jeans off.

For some reason, this afternoon they were both in a very kissy mood. Sometimes they never once kissed while making love, while other times their fucking was filled with kisses. They were feeling affectionate and played with each other's pubic hair and giggled a lot while slowly becoming more and more aroused. He went to plunge his fingers into her when she stopped him.

"I don't want to stop and unpack the lube," she said with a laugh.

"Lazy."

She climbed on top of him and slowly lowered herself onto his cock. He let out a loud sigh—she always felt so good to him. His hands rested on her thighs as she ground back and forth on him. It had taken her a while to relearn her body's responses after menopause, but she'd eventually come to an understanding that as long as she accepted that her body was different, and had patience with herself (and her lovers), sex was richer than before.

Sometimes she liked to teeter on the edge of orgasm, knowing it would be more like an escalator going down than a plunge off a cliff, subtle and almost missed if she wasn't paying attention. But today there were people to meet and places to be, so she let her mind wander to its darkest corners where the quick orgasms lived, and soon was there. She bit her lip to keep from crying, since she knew that Gerald could misinterpret her sex tears. He pumped into her faster and faster, and just as she got ready to shift position for him, he came, shuddering.

"I think I like this bed better than the one when we were here last. That was creaky and I was constantly afraid someone would hear us. Especially later in the week."

They'd just finished getting dressed for the evening when Gerald said this. Jillian looked at him and smiled. He was dressed in his authorly outfit and looked quite staid. While she was dressed a little more flamboyantly, as befitted her reputation, they still both looked their age.

"Plus it has way more room."

THE DEACON

Tahira Iqbal

Mark Deacon, the billionaire head of a legendary hotel empire, is holding the room in the palm of his hand. He's dressed in black trousers, a crisp white shirt, embodying the casual style that he'd asked us to all adopt today via a company-wide memo. From the elevated podium, he delivers a genuine, praise-filled speech about the impending opening of his latest hotel and the effort it's taken from the men and women standing before him.

He's more handsome than I expected…which is a strange thing to think because we've only ever communicated via email. I'd been brought onto the project in the late stages of the build, and curiosity had me searching for images of him online, but the man was surprisingly camera shy.

"You've all done a fantastic job," he says, white teeth showing against his true, easy smile. "We open in one month, so today, let's enjoy the facilities as if we were guests, take notes; anything, no matter how big or small, good or bad, I want them submitted to my PA by the end of the day. We're going to make the Deacon the best place to stay in town!"

Rapturous applause breaks out; the room and I are all charmed as he heads off the stage to the floor, shaking hands with a few of the construction crew.

His PA, at his side, whispers something in his ear and he politely makes his way from the men, snaking through the throng toward the back of the hall and...me.

I get azure eyes that darken once he sees me. Immediately, there's a rolling heat unfurling within my system that makes my heartbeat rise so much that I can actually hear it in my ears. He's six foot plus of pure presence, totally suave, and the women around me are staring. Yes, our boss is actually that good looking.

"Leila?" the PA says, "Have you got a minute? I'd like for you to officially meet the man who hired you!"

I smile at the PA who'd arranged my first few days here, then focus my attention on reaching for his waiting hand, his smile dazzling, much like the diamond-studded watch he's wearing.

"Mr. Deacon."

I have to blink back the charge in my system as we touch.

"Please call me Deacon, I prefer that." He says warmly, "Leila, it's a pleasure to finally meet you, I'm sorry that it's not been before today."

"That's okay; I think we've done fine over email." His cologne, a stunning, expensive scent, winds around my senses, easily elevating my pulse to a rolling thunder.

His PA hands me a file marked PRIVATE AND CONFIDENTIAL.

"I'd like to go over the security for one of the penthouse floors," Deacon says.

I go cold as I rifle through the papers and schematics. "I thought everything was okay?" I must look worried because he says, "It's nothing to be wildly concerned about, but we do need to address something." He reaches for his ringing phone. "I noted a blind spot that I'd like for us to check. Our previous security contractor wasn't as good as you, so I'd like to chat through it. How's three p.m. on penthouse level three?"

He tips his head in a parting greeting, walking away on his call, his PA in tow after she confirms the meeting by sending me a meeting request via email that makes my BlackBerry buzz in my pocket.

I'm a perfectionist and so is Deacon, apparently. We'd exchanged hundreds of emails about security; he really knew this place inside out and considering how many ventures he had around the world; the thirty-two-year-old was seriously on the ball.

I'd been hired right off the back of a job in L.A., flown first class and set up in an apartment the very next day at his request.

I merge with the crowds onto the carpeted mezzanine level that overlooks the spectacular glass-roofed reception, aiming for the lazy, looping staircase that will take people to the drinks waiting for them below.

Great... I had hoped that I would have been able to enjoy the hotel along with everyone else, but now I'm going to be working. I lift out my phone, call the spa, and cancel the manicure I'd promised myself for weeks now.

I walk to my office located in the basement of the hotel, which is more like a mini subterranean city. Staff walk purposefully along the corridors, some aiming for the large catering kitchens, others finalizing the notices and signs that will ensure we don't get lost in this lair (like I did for the first week). The housekeeping department has been prepping rooms all month and I dodge a giant stack of fluffy white towels being wheeled toward a large service elevator.

I push open the glass doors to the main security hub after swiping my pass against the reader. The room looks like something that NASA would launch a shuttle from; rows of desks, each with its own computer, all facing a bank of over one hundred high-definition screens that show me every inch of the hotel. Or so I thought.

I open the file, take out the papers and plans, tie back my dark shoulder-length hair and take a deep breath.

There was a minor catch in reception, due to the support columns holding up the mezzanine but I'd compensated for that by installing cameras above the front doors that my predecessor hadn't bothered to do…but Deacon had been talking about the penthouse levels, specifically level three.

I check the plans again, but don't see anything.

After two hours, I'm frustrated and hungry as I'd barely had time for breakfast and my run this morning. I stuff the documents back into the file as Kelly, one of my security managers, arrives,

"Damn, that spa is something else!" she says. "I got a manicure for the staff party tonight." She flashes me blood-red nails. "Hey, who stole your apple?"

I lift the file. "Deacon says there's a blind spot on one of the penthouse floors." Kelly stops smiling, "Would you look through this?" I hand her file. "I'm going to get some food, and then I'll head back."

"Leila, you're the best in the country, you don't miss anything. We should have hired you right off the bat."

"Yeah, you should have." I sigh wearily, rising from my seat.

"Hey, that Deacon guy, he's kinda something, right?" Kelly fans herself theatrically with the file.

The attraction I'd felt earlier stirs. Eyes the color of rich seas. Charisma that hits like a punch.

"He's something all right."

I arrive at the second floor restaurant where a casual lunch is being served. The space is a noisy cavern as I join the buffet line, chatting to a few colleagues as I collect my food. I avoid the elegantly presented dessert mountain, but make eye contact with the giant ice sculpture of the hotel that mirrors the spectacular knife-shaped tower to perfection.

I take a moment, plate in hand, to appreciate the view beyond the huge windows that overlook the man-made beach, the expansive spa and the winding trails that lead to the private two-story villas in the grounds of the hotel.

I hear a deep laughter from somewhere to my right…Deacon, at a large table, sleeves rolled up to his elbows, his dark hair catching the sunlight coming through the glass. He says something funny and the people around him laugh with real enthusiasm.

I get a funny knot in my stomach when he excuses himself from his companions and then weaves his way through the diners toward me.

"Leila, have you had a chance to look through my notes?"

I take a small breath; plaster a smile.

"Yes, I have. I'm just getting a colleague to go through them as well, to make sure we really haven't missed anything. I'm not quite sure where the blind spot is, so our meeting will be helpful."

"Good, I think you and I both know that the person who did the work before you…"

"Wasn't me."

Deacon appraises me; lips first, then eyes.

"He certainly wasn't."

The room fades away suddenly. It's just him. Those vibrant eyes. Still fixed on me.

There's a wonderful crash of heat in my pelvis.

"Enjoy your lunch, Leila," Deacon says, heading back to his table, a smile on his lips.

I'm at my desk, Kelly with me. "I think I know what he's talking about…" she says, turning one of the plans toward me. "Look, do you see anything strange?"

I assess the plan and then flick the papers looking at penthouse levels one and two. My shoulders slump. "The camera on level three… It's in the wrong friggin' place." I press a finger to the paper. "That's why I missed it, because it's exactly like that in the corridor and on the plans, so technically there's no mistake…" I groan, moving my finger. "We'd have a full field of vision if the camera was here." I point to the position directly opposite from where it has been installed. "How did I miss it?"

"You didn't, because the plans are an exact match to the installation, so the problem isn't actually highlighted," Kelly says. "Deacon did a walk-through about three months ago, flagged up the issue, because he's built a million of these places…"

"He knows the layout better than anyone." I say.

"Yeah, I guess so, but he's just being…"

"Hey, when it's eight billion dollars of your own money on the table, you're allowed to nitpick," I interject, leaning back in my chair, taking the papers with me. "I better go check it out." I reach for a walkie-talkie that's sitting in the base unit, then hand one to Kelly, adjusting the settings as I do. "I'll let you know when I'm there."

I exit the lift nearly seventy stories up, walking into a freshly decorated corridor that still smells like wet paint.

"Leila to Kelly."

Static, then Kelly's clear voice comes through,

"I've got you on the screen; you're in the north corridor."

There are only four penthouse suites on each floor; each one nearly ten thousand square feet of stunning, opulent, no-holds-barred luxury.

I walk to the end of the corridor before turning a sharp right and stopping at the first penthouse door.

"Can you see me?"

"Negative."

I press the walkie-talkie into my forehead; curse something under my breath as I look at the dome-shaped camera at the end of the hallway in question. I step forward, away from the doorjamb and two feet into the corridor.

"I've got you now."

"I shouldn't have missed this."

"Leila, you've been dealing with the beachfront security for the last three weeks."

"Yeah, and no tan to show for it."

Kelly laughs, I don't.

"Right, this means we're going to have to get some remodeling done ASAP and I need to fix the plans with the architect as soon as possible." I mentally pick out the spot on the wall where the camera should be reinstalled.

"Want me to email the tech guys? Plan the work?"

"No, we can do it later, why ruin their day?" I check out the corridor again and then hit the talk button. "I'm going to stay here for a while, make some of my own notes. Over."

"Okay, take your time. Kelly out."

I lift out my master key and slide it into the reader, entering the penthouse. I'm instantly impressed by the wide windowpanes that show me a bright city that stretches for miles. The living area has angular wooden tables, low white leather sofas and rugs on the hardwood floor. The private decked terrace, accessed through the bi-fold doors, is devoid of any furniture;

a design fault with the customized table and chairs had pushed back the delivery to later this week.

I take a seat at the desk, lift out a sheet of headed notepaper from the letter rack and lift the complimentary pen. I quickly sketch the corridor. The suites have already attracted some high-profile bookings…it's eighteen grand a night to stay here and for that you get luxury amenities, a twenty-four-hour butler and a pick-up from the airport in a custom Phantom. And if something went wrong…it would be on my watch, so Deacon was right to pick up on it.

I lift out my buzzing phone, deactivating the reminder for my meeting in thirty minutes.

Feeling annoyed, I head to the window, watching the world go by. It really is a stunning day, giving everyone at the poolside the best weather to enjoy the water.

Twenty minutes later, I visually double check and establish that the problem is only on level three after checking each floor just in case.

I reach for my phone to check the time, but realize that I've left it in the suite.

"Kelly, what time is it?" I say into the walkie-talkie as I head into the stairwell, going up; it had been faster to use the stairs to get to each floor rather than waiting for the elevator.

"Five to three."

"I'm just going into my meeting with Deacon."

"See you when I see you," Kelly says and we end our conversation.

A few minutes later, I have my phone and I'm just doing my final checks when Deacon rounds the corner alone.

There's a quickening of my breath and circling heat that creates a sensational heaviness within.

"You were right," I say in a rush. "About the blind spot."

He takes my paper drawing, our fingers briefly touching.

I watch him as he appraises it, nodding to himself as he reads my comments.

"Okay," he says with a smile. "Why don't you walk me through it?"

I guide Deacon through the area of concern, highlighting the problem with the location and the odd angles that have been created by the mix-up on the plan and therefore the installation. I also succinctly plot through the solution and assure him that I'll get it fixed as soon as possible.

"I'm really sorry that I missed it."

"Hey, you've been working flat out; we've caught it now, so don't worry. Show me again," he says. "The exact spot."

I reach for my walkie-talkie, gesturing for him to walk to the first corner.

"Leila to Kelly, come in."

"Go ahead."

"I'm with Deacon, can you confirm the moment you lose us." We walk side by side to the suite; I motion for Deacon to step toward me as I press myself against the door.

We're inches apart.

"Negative," Kelly says. "I don't see either of you."

"Thanks, Kelly." I end the conversation there and put the walkie-talkie into my back pocket, growing more unsteady from his proximity. The fine cotton of his shirt brushes my fingertips.

Deacon raises his hand, pressing it to the door just above my head, as if to box me in. His gaze roves my features, lips parting in a sexy smile that warms me along with the pounding force between my legs that's been gathering pace since I saw him this morning. I'm fascinated by the shadows playing across his eyes.

"So," he says in a rough whisper, "If I was to fuck you, right here, no one would see?"

A serious shiver flickers down my spine as my breath jumps. "I guess not."

With a slow teasing slide, Deacon unzips my denims. I drag in a breath as his hand disappears, cupping the cotton of my panties. I sigh in exultation as he slides a finger...there.

"You're wet." His lips are against my ear, sending his breath cascading down my neck. "I like that."

He presses harder, dragging a moan out of my throat. I part my legs, needing the wider stance for stability. I tip my head back, resting against the door. There's a hitch in my senses, a marching heat that makes me pant softly against the tingles that are bouncing over my lady nerves.

"That's it..." His finger swipes harder, back and forth, over the soft, soaked material. He parts my lips with his tongue, probing, checking me out and leaving me quivering. I'm suddenly on the edge, getting there fast with reckless abandon. Deacon removes his hand,

"Fuck..." he says roughly. "I need you now."

With quick hands, he unbuckles his belt, pulls down his zipper, shoving his trousers and boxers down his hips. Then he's inside of me and what follows is a hard, fast, stunning hurricane of eroticism that has me biting my lip to stop from screaming.

We both come within seconds, my abs hurting from the power of his possession.

His forehead goes to mine, his breathing heavy as he slows his thrusts. I hold him, dazed by the sensations.

"Open the door," he whispers, sliding out of me.

I do, with shaking hands.

"Upstairs. Now."

In the loft-style master suite, Deacon hauls off his shirt, revealing sleek muscles under tan skin. He slides his belt off, throwing it to the side of the room before reaching for my denims, pushing them down my thighs. I get out of them and my sneakers as he takes the hem of my shirt, tugging it over my head.

My bra and panties join his belt as the hunger builds; the fire in his eyes charges me as he strips fully.

Deacon plants a kiss hard on my lips as he winds a hand around my waist, dragging me to him, his hard cock sliding in between my legs but not in, just along the wetness.

We tumble to the bed; my nipples are hard, pointed, and he latches on to them, applying pressure that sends a new surge of wetness down my inner thighs. Kisses go to the nape of my neck as he settles over me, guiding his length inside of me.

I surrender to him fully in this room that is nothing more than a glass-fronted cube looking into the sky.

"Deacon..." I gasp, electrified by his spectacular force that has me keeping a death grip on the fine linens. Blood ignites within, sending me screaming headlong into a bone-shattering orgasm that arches me like a bow.

Deacon weaves his fingers into my hair after undoing the practical ponytail. He keeps me close, thrusting in, pulling out, delighting me with the delicious melody he's creating, one that's got him muttering curses and prayers in equal measure.

Then silence.

Nothing but skin on skin.

The slick snaps of moisture.

Deacon flies into an orgasm that brings him to my breast with force. My own release is a spectacular burning firecracker that roars from the heart of me.

He brings his lips to the shell of my ear. "There's a party tonight in the nightclub for everyone," he says breathlessly. "I'm going to make an appearance. You"—he kisses my temple—"meet me here, eight p.m."

I watch him get dressed and then get a deep and decadent kiss from him before he jogs down the stairs and leaves the suite.

I get up; jelly legged and aiming for the minibar. I grab a bottle of water, downing it in gulps.

I pull my clothes on, then find my walkie-talkie.

"Leila to Kelly."

"Hey girl… Have you been running?"

I take a second to breathe as I sink back on the ruffled five-hundred-thread-count sheets.

"So, just to confirm, that blind spot really is there…"

Silence, then, "Yes, it's there. Wait… I see Deacon… He's heading to the elevator now."

My body trembles at the thought of him, the naughty moment we've just shared, the promise of tonight.

"What's he looking so happy about?" Kelly says. "The man's grinning from ear to ear."

I press the talk button, feeling the heat of the sun on my face as it comes through the windows. "Hey, I can't make the party tonight," I say, fighting a smile and enjoying the delicious ache between my thighs. "You're going to have to go by yourself."

LOVE, LOUD AS A BOMB

Steve Isaak

It wasn't just the seaquake or the impending tsunami that drove Carl Sims to head to higher ground.

It was Anya.

Immediately after the tsunami warnings, blasted from radios and televisions, Anya had called him on his cell phone and said, "See? I told you that it would happen. I'm at the Inn, room two-twenty-four."

"I was already packed and on my way," he said. He made a right turn off the main island highway. "Just in case your dreams were right."

"They weren't wrong before," she said. "*Now* do you believe I'm psychic?"

But that was small, could've-gone-either-way stuff, Carl thought. He didn't say that, though.

"Yes," he replied. "I'll be there in a few minutes."

"Okay." He heard the smile, the edge to her voice, reflecting his own urgency: they were going to fuck. Finally.

He turned off his hands-free speakerphone and increased his speed, blasting past lush, animal-silent jungle lands toward the Mountain Inn, atop the central mountain that loomed over Main Island.

I'm lucky to date a girl who has freaky future dreams, where nobody gets hurt, he chuckled. *In ten minutes, this highway is going to be packed.*

The geophysicist at the Pacific Tsunami Warning Center in Hawaii, thousands of miles away, had dispatched a bulletin to the Main Island authorities, who, without delay, had alerted its five hundred citizens and tourists. According to the authorities, the tsunami was going to breach Main Island and its archipelagic neighbors in thirty minutes.

Traffic was already forming behind him. Two green camouflage military trucks with troops in back and a military jeep passed him.

Almost there.

His crotch tingled in anticipation as he imagined what would likely transpire when he arrived at their hotel room: Anya's sexy, slender-girl body and relatively large breasts unveiled to him for the first time, because she'd wanted their first day-long fuck to coincide with the spectacular fruition of one of her disaster-based visions.

Further imaginings of her taking him into her lovely little mouth instantly brought him to half hardness.

Slow down, brother, he reminded himself, shifting in his seat. *You're not there, yet.*

Up ahead, the mountain's shadow blocked out the faint gray of clouded sunlight. His brown button-down shirt still stuck to him, but a cool breeze had replaced the humid heat.

The curvy asphalt road rose toward the box-like hotel, where Anya, pepper hot and raring to go, awaited him.

They'd met at the Beach Bar, where a mutual friend, a writer like Carl, had introduced them. Anya worked there as a waitress. She'd barely paid attention to him, mistaking his friendly smile for yet another customer come-on, until he'd put on one of her favorite songs, "Sea of Love."

Their eyes had met—his light gray, hers dark—across the bar when they both realized they were singing it under their breaths, a sparking moment.

The rest, as they say, was history.

The wind became stronger as his jeep approached the mountain's crest. Just beyond this last rise lay the Inn, as locals called it.

Not everyone would be going to the Inn. Two lesser mountains flanked it, mountains that should prove high enough to avoid the tsunami's flooding. He glanced toward the mountain on his right, where military personnel were setting up the disaster relief camp, a large, round-dome hall with bathrooms, beds, food, medical supplies and other necessities.

He parked in the half-empty parking lot in front of the six-story hotel. Grabbing his duffel bag off the front passenger seat, he got out of his jeep and locked it. Cooling winds hit him, briefly freezing his sweaty body.

I'll be hot inside her, he chuckled, walking fast toward the hotel. He glanced up at its second story, hoping to see Anya, though he doubted he would.

He didn't.

He passed through the open, sliding doors of the Inn. Carl smiled at the clerk behind the registration desk—Ian, who, like Carl, was a stateside transplant who loved his mojitos—before continuing toward the elevators. Ian was on the phone, frowning.

The large, tropical-themed lobby was half full of people,

most of them calm. A few looked concerned, particularly the sun-reddened tourists. Many of the people here, including Carl, Anya and Ian, had experienced tsunamis before: they were property-disastrous, but, with proper warnings, insurance and effective evacuation, not life-threatening.

He pressed the UP button for the elevator. A moment later, the light above lit and dinged. Stepping back, he let five or so passengers exit before getting on it himself. He had the elevator to himself.

He tapped the second-floor button, and the elevator rose for a few seconds, stopped, settled and dinged. The double doors slid open and he exited.

"Two oh five, two oh seven..." He walked down the green-carpeted, gold-brown hall to the room Anya had rented for them and knocked on the door. "It's open," he heard Anya say faintly. He opened the door and stepped inside.

The first thing he saw was Anya in a sash-tied silky robe that showed off her long native-tan legs. Her nipples, large and dark, poked through the thin material covering them. She stood near the sliding glass door that led to their step-out balcony, facing him. Around her, faint sunlight filtered into the golden-brown room with the king-sized bed.

"You made it," she said lightly.

He wasn't fooled by her voice. He could see the impatience, the wantonness in her dark eyes.

After setting his duffel bag in the open closet, he went to her.

They embraced and kissed passionately. She unbuttoned and unzipped his cargo shorts, pressing herself against his erection.

"My shoes," he said, breaking away from her.

"Fall back on the bed," she said, and smiled.

He did as she said. The bed bounced him slightly when he hit it.

Stripping off her flimsy robe, she dropped it on the floor. She got on the bed, placed her wet, neatly trimmed pussy above his face, and lowered her mouth to his florid erection, her right hand working his shaft.

She sighed and groaned as he began tonguing her spread, dark sex. Gripping her thighs, he pulled her lower to him so he could lick her better, push his tongue deeper into her glistening, flushed tanginess.

His grip on her became tighter. So did his balls.

"I'm about to come," he gasped.

She laughed, took his jism in her mouth, on her lower face. He continued licking her, though his tongue action had lost some of its focus.

Slapping his hands off the back of her thighs, she said, "I'll reposition myself." She laughed again. "You almost gave me 'pirate eye.'"

She sat on the edge of the bed, wiping her face with tissues while he untied and took off his shoes and the rest of his clothes.

"S'okay. In a few minutes, I'm going to come in your mouth," she continued. "And when I come, it'll be when the first wave hits Main Island."

She pulled him to her as they stepped out onto their balcony to watch the scene below. Their mutual heat and stickiness caused his dick to stir.

She brushed her fingers along it and kissed him.

The main highways, which branched out onto the three mountains, were jam-packed with cars. From where they were, Carl and Anya could see an end to their line.

Beyond the roads, beyond the landmass, the sea had risen, but not to its full tsunami height. It looked close, though.

"They're going to make it," she reassured him. "There was enough advance warning. And there would've been more, if the authorities had believed me when I first warned them about this."

"One of them—Alan—did," he reminded her, running his hands over her thighs in a tickling fashion. She shuddered pleasurably.

"He was voted down," she replied. "No biggie. Do me."

She reentered the room, lay on the bed and spread her legs.

He knelt down and resumed tonguing her tangy, dewy and slightly bitter sex, where his dick had rubbed against her. Her dark-edged, flushed-red lips were exposed to his focused, erotic ministrations, her hands in his short sweaty hair. His hands and fingers sought out and pinched her hard nipples, causing her to close her thighs around his tang-slicked face.

She came the first time, groaning and shuddering, ten minutes later.

Lowering her legs onto the bed, he laid the side of his face against her thigh.

"I know you didn't come," she said. "I also know you're fully erect. Now fuck me like I've wanted you to all these weeks."

Sweaty and chuckling, he got up and slid inside her clenching wetness as she spread her legs farther apart.

Four minutes later, she sighed, quaked and came before he did, whispering, "Boom," in his ear, just as the first wave hit the island with a dull thunderous sound.

NIGHT SCHOOL

Valerie Alexander

Working the night shift at a small-town hotel is the ideal job for introverts. At city hotels, there are valets, bellhops and room service attendants in the lobby at any hour of the night. But at the Midwestern off-highway chain hotel where I worked as the night auditor, the silence was broken only by the sound of distant ice machines and the hum of the computer printing out the guest folios.

And the comings and goings of the escorts, of course.

I was three hours into my shift when the glass doors opened and the youngest of the usual male escorts came in. "Hey, Nina," Dalton said. As always, his smile at seeing me behind the desk seemed genuine. Not that it meant anything. He didn't see me that way. Most men didn't.

I waved casually, as if I hadn't been hoping that he would have a date in the hotel tonight. "Hi."

He sauntered to the elevator, pressed the button and leaned against the wall at the perfect angle to show off his long, snake-hipped body. It had to be a gift, knowing how to showcase himself like that. As usual, he was dressed in black with his dark-blond hair artfully rumpled. Dalton tended to show up for most of his dates looking like a knockoff James Dean, though I'd seen him wear everything from polo shirts to basketball jerseys to suits before. I assumed those were client requests.

The elevator pinged and the doors opened. He flashed me a heart-melting smile and got on. As soon as the doors closed, I checked my reflection. My red ponytail was in a state of collapse and the shadows of insomnia circled my eyes. Oh, well. He didn't notice my looks anyhow.

I'd never seen myself falling for a male escort. I'd never seen myself falling for a pretty boy at all, let alone a twenty-year-old who seduced men and women for a living. I'd been scoffing at handsome men for as long as they'd been ignoring me. All cats are gray in the dark, I would say to my friends. And I wanted to believe that. But here I was, swooning over a professionally devastating smile. It was mortifying.

I wondered who Dalton was seeing tonight and what they would do. I knew most of his clients were men, though he saw couples and the occasional woman, too. He was open with me about what he did—once he'd figured out that I didn't care about his doing business in the hotel, we'd fallen into the habit of chatting after his dates. But he never shared too many details. I wished he would. I wanted to picture it; wanted to know how he took off his clothes, if he did it slowly with a boyish smile, or if his clients preferred to unwrap him like a gift. I wanted to know his techniques for pleasing clients; if he was better at being forcefully passionate or tender and sensitive. I wanted to know if he preferred men or women.

I wanted to know what it would be like if I hired him. If he would stammer and get uncomfortable, or if he would shrug and go to work. I wanted to know how I would feel paying for sex from someone who wasn't attracted to me. If feeling his hard warm body against mine, his cock mine to command, would compensate for his lack of interest.

And I really wanted to know what it was like to be so hot that people paid money to fuck you. I wasn't homely, but I *was* invisible—the girl who got overlooked, the girl for whom the friend zone was invented. At twenty-six, I'd long since made my peace with this. But Dalton's frequent nocturnal visits to the hotel made me aware that sexual magnetism and money were just different kinds of currency, and that I had little of either.

One hour went by and then another. Dalton was still up there. That was unusual. He rarely spent the night with anyone and worked mostly in one- or two-hour shifts.

Almost three hours after his arrival, the soft ping of the elevator sounded. He walked into the lobby looking defeated and annoyed. To my delight, he came straight for the desk.

"Bad night?" I asked.

"Horrible," he said. "I hate clients like her. They don't know what they want and no matter what you do, it's never enough."

Her. A small spurt of jealousy went through me for that woman who'd just had three naked hours with Dalton. "Nothing you can do about that, I guess."

"Well…" He hesitated and gave me a disturbed look. "Okay, I'm just going to ask. When a woman says she wants to be dominated, what the hell is she expecting?"

It was all I could do not to laugh. "Hasn't anyone requested that before?"

"Yeah, all the time. And they love it. I hold their arms down over their head, pull their hair, tell them what a dirty girl they are… I've even spanked them before." He looked defiant.

Sometimes I forgot how young he was. "Dalton, that's how

vanilla women like to be dominated. Submissive women are a different story. I'm guessing your client was a sub."

A frown creased his brow. Apparently even professional sex workers weren't always versed in BDSM. "Okay, so what do subs want?"

"Some want you to degrade them. Some want you to control them or punish them, or just bind and tease them with sensation. They're all different. But mostly they want you to take over."

"And how do you know so much about it?"

I leaned back in my chair, locked eyes with him and smiled. He got it.

"Wow." He looked away from me, embarrassed. I wondered if it made him uncomfortable to think about me sexually, his front-desk pal.

"Okay." He pushed his disheveled hair back. "So tell me what to do. I tried everything and she just laughed at me."

Poor Dalton. "There isn't a secret formula. Like I said, everyone's got different triggers."

"Nina, this is my job," he said with real anguish. "I can't be laughed at. Help me out."

"I...I can't. Seriously, it's something you have to feel."

He leaned his arms on the desk and looked in my eyes. "My whole job is about faking things I don't feel," he said pointedly.

True. But I still didn't want to propose the obvious. "You could try watching some domination porn."

"Or you could teach me." He looked hesitant.

Something fluttered deep in my gut. He had suggested it. It was his idea.

"Okay," I said. My voice was weak. I was always afraid of jinxing it when I was about to get what I wanted.

* * *

The next night I met Dalton at the hotel two hours before my shift. I'd already gotten the key for the room and taken it offline so it couldn't be assigned to a guest. Initially, he'd suggested my apartment, but the thought made me a little squirmy. I didn't know if I could transition from seeing him naked in my bed to casually greeting him at work again. And the truth was that the idea of conducting a kinky lesson upstairs in the hotel while none of my coworkers knew I was on the premises was kind of exciting. So we met at a side door and took the back elevators up to the third floor.

Oddly, he seemed more nervous than I was. I couldn't imagine why, given that he met strangers for sex for a living. Hotels were as much his workplace as mine.

He tapped my bag. "What's in there?"

"Tools." I hadn't brought anything too advanced, but I was curious how he'd react to them. "Just basic stuff."

The elevator stopped and we got out and walked down the green-and-gold-patterned corridor. Next to me, Dalton seemed even taller than I'd thought.

"So am I going to need a whole kit for this kind of job?"

"I would think the clients would provide their own toys, but you'd know that better than me." I opened the door.

The thrill of erotic anticipation flooded me as I took in the dual queen beds, oak bureau and matching table. The generic blandness and sterility seemed as always like a sanctum of anonymity, a promise that any sex here meant nothing as soon as the door closed at checkout time. It was why I loved hotel rooms. The utter lack of history and context seemed to make it possible to transform into the woman I wanted to be.

My hands were shaking. To keep him from noticing, I tossed the bag on the bed and began to unpack it. Out came the nipple clamps, the spreader bar, the paddle and the cuffs. Dalton watched with fascination. "Christ, look at all this kinky stuff."

I couldn't hold back. "Dalton, you're a pro. How can you be shocked by all this? Don't you see freaky stuff all the time?"

"Not really," he said. "Most of my clients want your basic suck and fuck. You'd be surprised how boring escorting can be."

He was right—I was surprised. "But what about your regular sex life?" I asked curiously. "What kind of sex are you into?"

Dalton looked startled, then blushed and sat on the other bed. "Nothing. I mean, just regular stuff."

It sounded like I'd found a sensitive spot. Interesting. But I didn't probe. Instead I pulled my T-shirt over my head and unsnapped my bra, letting it fall to the floor.

I sat down topless on the bed, facing him. He looked at my nipples, then quickly looked away again. It was incredible how shy he was being, unless this was an act.

I held out the clamps. "Put these on me."

"They look like they'd hurt."

"Dalton, just put them on me."

As he fumbled with the clamps, I began our first lesson. "It's a myth that BDSM is all about hard-core pain. Some people are into that, but for most of us it's about sensation and power exchange. Here, screw it a little tighter…it's okay…right, like that."

He stared at my nipples. They were flushing a darker pink now. "How does that feel?"

"It's more about how it will feel later. When you take them off, my nipples will be so sensitive you can make me come just touching them."

He laughed awkwardly and ducked his head.

"Dominate me," I ordered him.

"What?"

"Just give it your best shot. Tell me what to do, order me around."

He got to his feet. For one comical moment, he raised his index finger as if he were going to scold me. "Take off your pants."

His tone wasn't exactly masterful. I got up and stepped out of my jeans and panties, then sat back down. He loomed over me as if thinking about what to do next. "Now what?"

I suppressed a sigh. "Look, Dalton, I know you don't actually want me, but pretend that you do. Tell me to spread my legs and show you my pussy. Tell me to finger myself, or get on all fours. Grope me. Tell me you're going to do whatever you want to me because I'm just a little slut and there's nothing I can do to stop it."

The color in his face deepened and he began to laugh nervously. "I would feel ridiculous saying all that. I mean, when you say it, it sounds good but…"

Then I understood the problem. I stood up and took off the nipple clamps.

"We're doing this wrong," I told him. "A lot of people believe you have to submit before you can dominate. So I'm going to show you, okay?"

He ran a hand through his hair and laughed again. Was I imagining the relief in his voice? "Okay."

"Take off your clothes. All of them."

Now he was on familiar ground. Dalton backed up and began to pull off his shirt. He looked at the wall with this weird smile and I realized just how embarrassed he really was. I was the one whose presence had been requested tonight and he was the one who had done the requesting. He didn't know who was the client here, him or me, and the ambiguity had robbed him of his usual confidence.

His body was my idea of perfect—lean and sinewy, with a nicely sculpted chest and hard stomach. I held my breath as he pushed down his jeans. Good Christ, his cock was big: long and thick and a bit veiny, outsized in comparison to his narrow hips.

"Good boy." I tried not to let my voice betray the excitement rampaging through me. "Now stand still."

I stood up and walked a slow circle around him. I was dying to know when he'd gotten hard: when I got naked or when I began to dominate him. I supposed it didn't matter, though the first would have been a nice compliment. "Lock your hands on the back of your neck."

His long back arched as he obeyed. I ran one fingertip down his spine, then cupped his ass. He had surprisingly round cheeks given his sinewy build and—oh, yes—they were virgin pale. He'd never been spanked, not recently at least, and I suspected not ever.

My heart raced. I reminded myself to play this out properly.

I stroked his thighs. He shivered. We hadn't negotiated limits or talked about safewords; in fact, we hadn't even talked about how much sex this instruction would actually involve, but his stiff cock was dark with engorgement, his balls were tight, and a pearly web of precome gleamed in the hotel lamplight. He was aching for this. It was written in his shaking thighs and the dazed mix of hope and entreaty in his eyes.

I slid my fingers over his balls and our gazes locked.

"Don't look me in the eye." I snapped my fingers near his face. "Look at the floor."

He obeyed. What a good boy. Even so, I pushed him down on the bed and hit his thighs lightly with the crop. "Open."

Dalton didn't even wince, suggesting he might enjoy a little sting on his skin, and spread his legs like he was showing off his big cock for a photo shoot.

I ran a light fingertip over his eyelids to close them. "Some subs like to be blindfolded," I explained, "and that might be something for you to consider with your clients. It's a form of sensory deprivation and it lets them pretend you're whoever they want."

"Okay..." He sounded confused by this sudden insertion of instruction.

I scratched my fingernails down his chest. He twitched. "And if you don't know how much pain they can take, find out by doing some tests on a scale of one to ten."

"Nina." His voice was hoarse. It sounded as if he was afraid I was going to retreat into professor mode and never deliver on this physical journey we'd started.

"Yeah?"

"What do you want me to do?"

Excellent question. I cropped him once more. "What I want is for you to lie there like my obedient pet boy and shut up. You don't move, you don't talk. You just lie there like a toy and let me use you, understand?"

"Yes, Mistress."

Mistress! We hadn't even discussed how he should address me and here he was sliding into sub space on his own. I was sure now that Dalton was passionately submissive by nature, good at pleasing his clients and obeying their requests, but no doubt dreaming of a sterner hand. I wondered how often he fantasized about this: sex where he was no longer responsible for the delivery but could lie back and be delivered to.

I got to work, locking his feet into the spreader bar and cuffing his wrists over his head. My stiff nipples were hot and my cheeks were flushed, and I could feel my wetness on the top of my thighs. All of my dreams about Dalton had been explicit, but in none of them had I even dared to hope for this much.

I sat on the bed and pulled him over my knee. That pale, sumptuous ass was trembling. I lightly smacked his right cheek with the paddle and he jumped. "Oh, come on now, that was nothing," I said. "You can take more than that."

I gave him a second smack on the left and he groaned. "I—oh, my god..." He clawed at the bedspread. So this was the fire at the heart of his secret fantasies: being spanked. I kept up a steady rhythm on those firm cheeks, the slap of the paddle in rhythm with his squirming on my lap. His erection was wedged between my bare thighs and as the spanking went on, he groaned harder, struggling to rub his cock against my skin.

Much as I enjoyed it, that just wouldn't do. I pushed him onto the bed.

"Is this what you want?" His green eyes looked half wild. I rubbed his cock until he was jerking and twisting on the bedspread, straining against his bonds. Okay, we were off script at this point. I wasn't really teaching him anything so much as exploiting the situation. But Dalton was panting and pushing his cock at me like he was begging for any part of me he could get.

I straddled his narrow hips, pushed his shaft against my thigh and spanked it. "You're my little bitch, aren't you?"

"Yes, Mistress."

I squeezed him until a soft guttural noise escaped him. "You're my toy to use however I please, aren't you?"

"Yes, yes, yes."

I pulled a condom out of my bag and wrapped up his dick, stroking him up and down my wet slit. The promise of him inside me was so good that my mouth was dry and I wanted to consume every inch of him. But I eased him in slowly, bit by bit, his enormous girth stretching my pussy walls. I'd always imagined mounting him and riding my way to heaven on his cock. The reality was a little more difficult. I balanced myself on his chest so I could control the depth of penetration. When he was lodged halfway inside me, I leaned over until my nipples just barely grazed his chest.

He gave a little grunt and tried to thrust into me deeper. I remained still, making him work for access. Even bound up, he used his hips like a pro, pushing a little deeper inside me with every thrust. It felt incredible, the sensation of his muscles twisting and straining beneath me just for the privilege of experiencing my pussy.

Dalton looked half drunk with lust now, his blond hair darkened with sweat. I reached beneath me and lightly stroked my clit. A warm whirlpool was building inside me, an insistent demand to sit all the way down on his cock, but there was a specific response I wanted from him first.

"Nina, *please*. Please just fuck me."

I loved being begged. A rush of euphoria shot through me and I moved back until I was completely enveloping his cock. This was the nexus of domination for me, being craved and needed so desperately that the enslaved boy at my feet lost all pride and control. A strangled noise of gratitude escaped Dalton as my pussy surrounded every inch of him, and I began to move and twist on top of him until he was bucking desperately beneath me.

"Don't stop," he cried. "Please, don't stop..."

I might have punished a different sub for such an outburst. But I knew Dalton's plea was born out of desperation, that we weren't mistress and sub or teacher and student anymore but us, Nina and Dalton, fucking our hearts out from a need that had been there all along. I leaned over and gripped his damp blond hair in my fists like the reins of a horse, and rode him with a vengeance. Our rhythm was urgent and primal now, his enormous cock ramming me into the most delicious kind of soreness. My every nerve was drowning in fire. He struggled beneath me against the cuffs and spreader bar, a spectacle of beautiful, bound helplessness, and as he groaned again, I began coming in mindless wet shudders. Dalton let go and followed suit, hips working furiously to pump out his orgasm.

When we caught our breath, I climbed off him and looked at the clock. Time to shower and get ready for the night audit. I unlocked Dalton.

He rolled over onto his stomach, shaking out his legs and arms. He didn't speak at first and I wondered if I had pushed him too far. Finally he got up and began to dress without meeting my eyes.

"Thanks," he said. "I have to say, I would never have guessed that you were submissive."

"I'm not."

He looked confused. "You said…"

"I didn't say anything. I smiled and you assumed."

Now he gave me a wary look of suspicion, as if I had tricked him. But he nodded finally and said, "You're hard to read, Nina… I admire that about you."

I knew he meant it as a compliment. "I'm sorry I didn't give you more pointers on how to dominate your clients," I said. "I suppose this wasn't that helpful."

He avoided my eyes again. "Yeah. We should probably do it a few more times, so I can take notes or something."

He scurried out without saying good-bye. I didn't let myself watch him vanish down the corridor past all those other rooms he had been inside before. Instead I fell back on the bed, reveling in my solitude in that generic hotel room, where everything was temporary and I could be anyone, and every secret wish granted was a stepping stone to transformation.

FEEL SO DIRTY

Andrea Dale

In the distance, I heard thunder.

My friends Amber and Jon had rented a vacation cottage on the beach, so the thunder was pretty much the only noise. That and the faint hum of the AC, which didn't do much to ease the stifling heat for me.

Rain would be nice, because I was sweltering. I'm a desert girl, not used to this southeast moistness. It was the heat *and* the humidity, thank you very much. Rain would at least cool things down.

Why I'd chosen to cross the country to visit them at this time of year was anyone's guess.

I'd already kicked off the covers, lying naked on the damp sheets, unable to sleep. If Amber hadn't had to rush back home because her sister's baby was making an early appearance, we'd be out on the porch now, sipping wine and giggling. But it was just Jon and me. I didn't know him as well as I did Amber, and although we'd shared a pleasant evening, we'd drifted off to our respective rooms an hour ago.

I didn't know Jon well, but…I felt a little guilty, sprawled here naked, my nipples beading at the thought of him. When I'd first met him, I'd dragged Amber aside and said, "*Damn,* he's fine!" and he was; oh, he was. Not just looks, either. Not just that he clearly worshipped my best friend. No, it was the sly grin, the vaguely flirtatious comments, the way he could make anything sound sexy as hell.

It didn't help that Amber had confided in me, as girls do, about how hot their sex life was. Jon was apparently solicitous and inventive in equal measure, as well as (according to Amber) sincerely aroused by her.

You know, in that "the way you touch me, I'll die if I don't come right now" kind of way.

Thunder growled again, a little louder.

I wasn't jealous; I loved Amber and was thrilled she'd found her Mr. Right.

That didn't stop me from fantasizing about her Mr. Right, unfortunately.

My brain warred with my conscience. I would never, ever hurt Amber. I'd been cheated on before. I knew what it felt like, and I loved her too much.

My skin was sticky in the heat, but my thighs felt stickiest of all. Was it cheating to just fantasize?

My body won out over my conscience. To assuage my guilt, I imagined a scenario where Amber and Jon had never dated, had become friends only.

Jon's smoky blue eyes would have caught mine across the room, and I would've moved toward him, hooked and reeled in by the erotic promise in his gaze.

I rolled my nipples between my fingers. Flashes of desire matched the flashes of lightning outside.

No, flash forward. I didn't want to go through the first-meeting crap—I wanted to fantasize about the sex.

I'd seen Jon without his shirt on; he had a fine dusting of dark hair along his chest. He wasn't overly buff, but his upper arms were muscled just the way I liked them. If he were stretched out over me, those muscles would flex as he held himself there, dipping his head down to tease me with kisses. First light, then devouring, our tongues clashing and our teeth knocking until we had to pull apart just to breathe.

My hips shifted restlessly, and I wished I'd brought my vibrator on the trip, but I could do just fine with my fingers—fingers I let trail down my belly, across my hips, just as I'd want him to do with hands and mouth, caressing and licking and biting. The pressure built in my clit, my pussy lips now slick with moisture. When I dipped my fingers in, I could smell my arousal, sweet and musky. Jon, I thought, would lick me and then kiss me so I could taste myself, and I brought my fingers to my mouth.

The thought of Amber flitted across my mind, but I pushed it away. This was just a fantasy, even if it was one that made my cunt clench with the deliciousness of it.

The visions muddled and blurred as I stroked my swollen clit. Legs parted, knees bent, I flicked it and pretended it was Jon's fingers doing so, Jon's talented tongue (for I knew it had to be). Just flashes of images: looking down to see his glossy dark hair, messy from the way I'd clutched his head, as he licked and sucked between my thighs. Jon rearing back over me, ordering me in a lust-rasped voice to wrap my legs around him. Positioning his cock just so, slipping and sliding it through my wetness, teasing me while I squirmed and begged beneath him and his eyes darkened and glinted with amusement at my desperation…so close…just there….

The sharp knock at the door almost made me scream. My

hips dropped against the bed. My clit pulsed in a faux orgasm, still on the brink, unfulfilled.

"Yeah?" I managed to say. My mouth was dry. I grabbed the sheet I'd kicked off, yanking it up over me, just in case.

"Everything okay?" Jon's voice came through the door.

Now I swallowed laughter. No, it wasn't okay. I'd just brought myself to near-ecstasy while thinking of him, and my groin ached from the denial of release.

"Um, fine, yeah. Why?"

"The storm's knocked out the power. Wanted to give you a flashlight."

I grabbed my robe from the tangled sheets at the foot of the bed. Belting it, I realized just how short and skimpy it was—I hadn't thought I'd need it except for dashes to the bathroom. I wiped my hand on the sheets and smoothed down my hair as best I could before I opened the door.

Oh, god. My stomach clenched and my thighs felt weak. Jon's hair was mussed, just like I'd fantasized, just as if I'd been pulling his head down to mine, my fingers tangled in the glossy black strands. As if I'd been riding him and his head tossed back and forth on the pillow in ecstasy.

He held out the flashlight. I grabbed it, trying to cover the fact that my hand shook.

"I'm sorry," he said with his half grin that furrowed the dimple in his cheek. "Air-conditioning's knocked out, too. You must be sweltering."

It really was as if my fantasy had come to life, because Jon was shirtless, wearing only a pair of loose running shorts, midnight blue like his eyes. His chest showed a sheen of sweat.

"It is a bit warm," I admitted, then wondered why he'd said it. Did I look disgustingly sweaty? Did I smell sweaty? Worse, did I smell like sex?

"I could use some lemonade," he went on, oblivious to my inner turmoil. "Want some? It's cooler out on the porch."

My mental panic continued. Hanging out on the porch with Jon, both of us nearly naked, would certainly help fuel my fantasies. But did my fantasies need any more fueling? Was this skirting the line of betraying Amber? Not to mention I was still aching with the need to come.

"Sure," I said finally. "Sounds great."

He lit candles, then disappeared inside for the drinks. It took me a few moments to arrange myself on the cushioned wicker chair in such a way that I didn't flash Jon when he returned with the lemonade. He was right: it *was* cooler here, with the barest hint of a breeze floating in on the electricity-charged air.

"I'm not used to this kind of weather," I commented, desperate for conversation. "Humidity, storms."

"It's always an adventure," he said. "It'll hit us before long, and the temperature will really drop. Keep your window open tonight; it'll help."

"When do you think we'll have power again?" The candles were too romantic, too perfect in the way they cast knife-edge shadows off his cheekbones.

"Probably be back on by the time we wake up," he said, and then I was thinking about waking up with him, spooned together, his hand over my breast and his morning cock thick against the crack of my ass, and...

Jon cleared his throat, and I jolted back to the present and realized why. My lemonade glass was sweating in the heat, dripping condensation onto my robe. A fraction of a second later I felt the chill as the water soaked in.

Of course, the drops were on the slope of my breasts. I glanced at him, but he was looking away now, intent on the candle flame. But he'd been watching.

I tried to diffuse the moment. "Feels good, actually."

Oh. That did the opposite. Plus it really did feel good. My nipples hardened, needy again, and I thought about taking my drink back to my room and putting the ice cubes to better use.

"Lea," Jon said suddenly. "This is...awkward."

"I'll go." I stood, grabbing the front of my robe when it threatened to slide open.

"No, it's okay," he said, also standing. "Look, you're a gorgeous woman, and I love that you and Amber are so close. I'd never do anything to affect that."

"I should hope not," I said, defensive and guilty in equal measure.

I'd told him, semi-drunkenly, at the reception that if he ever hurt Amber, I'd cut off his dick with a rusty spoon. I'd forgotten about that until now. Too busy having other thoughts about his dick, I guess.

"I just thought...no, it's stupid." He sat back down.

"What?" I mirrored his action, carefully, like before.

"I'd never cheat on Amber," he said, not looking at me. "But there's nothing wrong with a fantasy, is there?"

In the flickering candlelight, my cheeks flamed. "No," I said, wondering desperately if he knew.

"Would you be offended if I said I'd fantasized about you?"

What could I say to that but "I'd be flattered?" Then, clearing my throat, I added "Uh, the feeling's mutual, you know."

That grin again, glinting and gone. "Thanks. Glad to hear it."

Lightning flashed, and my skin seemed to hum with electricity.

"How about this," I said suddenly, crazily. "We'll go back to our rooms—separate rooms. Fantasize, masturbate. Knowing the other person is doing it."

"Are you sure...?"

"No talking about it, no telling each other what we're thinking about. That's going too far."

Of course, I wanted to know how he thought of us together. What positions, what acts went through his mind as he pulled on his cock. But at the same time, I didn't want to know—and imagining what he was thinking was kind of hot, too.

Plus I wasn't just toeing the line, I was kicking it off to one side.

Now it was his turn for his hand to shake; the ice rattled as he set his glass down. His shorts, I noticed, were tented, and I pressed my knees together against the sudden tremor in my groin.

"You're on," he said.

We seemed to press against opposite sides of the hallway as we made our way back to the bedrooms. As I turned to slip into mine, though, he swung close and whispered, "Leave your door open." Then he was gone.

The bedroom doors weren't within line of sight, but it still made sense; with the window and door open, I might catch a faint cross breeze.

I thought I knew, though, why he'd suggested it. It removed another barrier, even one we'd still never go past.

Before I turned off the flashlight, I fished a piece of ice from my near-empty glass of lemonade and, nestled against the pillows, did what I'd thought about on the porch.

My skin prickled as I circled the cold cube around my nipple, feeling it peak harder, tighter. I tweaked it with my fingers while I toyed the cube around my other nipple. Streaks of hot lightning tugged at my groin. I wished Jon were teasing me with the ice, making my nipples hard with the cold and then soothing them with the warmth of his mouth before biting down, throwing me off guard with pleasure and near pain.

When the fragment was almost melted, I dropped it between my breasts. It slid slowly down, nothing more than a tiny rivulet of water by the time it reached my navel.

What was he doing in his room? Did he toy with his own nipples, think of me sucking on them? Or had he gone straight for his cock, already hard? Did he imagine me sucking on him, licking him, cradling his balls in my hand, my hair spilling over and tickling his belly?

I scrabbled through the dark for the glass again, catching it just before it tipped and fell, and grabbed another piece of ice.

I spread my legs wide, tilted my hips and let the icy water drip, drip, drip onto my clit, each drop bringing me closer to the edge without letting me tip over. There was no reason to tease myself except to prolong my fantasy of Jon, as I imagined his hand wrapped around the purpling head of his cock, his fingers and shaft slick with lube and precome. His thighs straining, his head thrown back and the cords of his neck standing out as he…

That was it. I was done with teasing. I plunged my free hand down, found my throbbing clit, stroked. Heat and light bloomed in my belly as the contractions overtook me. I moaned, louder than I'd planned, and followed it with a grit-teethed "Fuck, yes," as I milked my orgasm just a few seconds longer.

From the other room I heard a hoarse cry, and realized my own sounds of passion had triggered his release. The knowledge sent my clit pulsing into a second climax.

That's why he'd wanted the doors open, I thought hazily, right before thunder boomed close by and the rain finally began to fall.

* * *

I woke the next morning to the smell of bacon. I hit a quick shower, still sticky from dried sweat and lemonade and come, and threw on a sundress that was deliberately long and loose.

"Morning," Jon said, handing me a plate of omelet and bacon and fruit. "Power's back on; hope it didn't bother you last night. Want to eat on the porch? It's a beautiful day."

I peered at him sideways as I poured myself some coffee. He sounded so casual, so ordinarily cheerful. I felt unbalanced, unsteady. Had I dreamed last night?

The feeling stayed with me when I saw that Jon's lemonade glass and the candles were gone from the porch. We'd promised not to talk last night, and it made sense to continue that into today (and, of course, beyond), but still...

Maybe it all *had* been a storm-induced fantasy. I hid my smile behind my steaming mug as we discussed my flight time that afternoon. If so, it had been a damn good one.

By the time I got home that night after a long, tiring flight, I had myself convinced it was nothing more than a fantastic hallucination. And I was able to coast on that thought through the next day's jet lag—until Amber called me.

Guilt churned in my gut as she apologized again for having to leave and told me about her new nephew. We were just about to hang up when she added, "By the way, I don't know what went on here, but I have to thank you. Jon's been a dynamo in bed since I got home tonight. I barely got away to call you."

"Nothing happened," I squeaked.

"Oh, I know you two didn't do anything," she said, laughing. "But Jon told me ages ago that he has fantasies about you. Must've been that skimpy robe of yours...and, I might add, he's right—you look *smoking* in it. So, thanks for the inspiration. Can't wait 'til you visit again!"

Before I could comment, she'd said good-bye and ended the call.

I stared at the phone for a long moment then reached for my vibrator.

Fantasies about Jon? Been there, enjoyed that. Fantasies about Jon and Amber?

Oh, I was just getting started with those.

PLEASE COME AGAIN

Tenille Brown

At night at the Misty Blue, Simone liked to prop the front doors of the hotel open and let the salty breeze from the ocean float in.

It was refreshing, and a lovely view, but it also kept her awake on the night shift because her coworker Henry was such a bore. That and the small radio she kept on the counter. But this time of night, all they played mostly were love songs, which didn't do Simone much good at all. If she'd *had* a man, this job certainly wouldn't have been conducive to maintaining the relationship.

Simone didn't live on the island. She rode the bus in for work. Ten to seven, that was her shift. She preferred it that way, because she was never one for crowds.

It wasn't a hard job, working the front desk. Simone mainly witnessed other people in their various stages of fucking: the anticipation, the noisy midst and the dreamy afterglow when they floated off the elevator hand in hand and checked out.

The residents didn't pass through much on the night shift

unless they were going for a night swim, and some of them did, but Simone was sure that wasn't all they were going to do.

Here on the tiny island, there were plenty of vacation hookups, but there were those other times when couples booked a room for a weekend or an overnight getaway.

Business was slow this time of year and it was getting cold, which was how Simone had met Randall. She'd seen him lingering around out front, and one night, on a break, she stepped outside and offered him a smoke.

Randall started coming around pretty regularly after that, and while Henry was on break, Simone would let him in.

The man was a stranger, this was true. He had no home, Simone knew this, too. But he was a pretty nice guy, if you got to know him. And Simone had gotten to know him quite well.

One night after their smoke, Randall had asked for a bar of soap. Simone had given it to him, no questions asked. She even offered him the lobby restroom to wash up.

Simone soon discovered she appreciated the company at night. Randall would sit in a lobby chair when business was slow and they would talk and laugh about the patrons at the hotel, and his buddies that roamed the streets like he did.

Simone gave Randall clothes that customers sometimes left behind. She'd even given him a beard trimmer and a small bottle of cologne.

Then she started letting him spend nights in the extra rooms upstairs. She would slip him in after Henry nodded off and out in the morning while Henry was making coffee.

Randall would be upstairs fast asleep by now.

Then, like lightning, it hit her. Simone hadn't given him his towels.

"I'll be right back," she said to Henry as she grabbed a stack and headed toward the elevator.

* * *

On the other side of the door, Simone could hear the shower. She used her master key card and let herself in.

The plan was to just leave the towels on the chair so Randall would have a fresh and dry one when he was done, and to leave just as quietly as she had come.

But Simone took a minute to take in the elegance of the room. It was nice. She tried to give him one of the nicer ones when she could. The bed in this one was king-sized and covered in white sheets. The carpet was beige plush. There was a sitting area and a flat-screen television. There was a coffeemaker with single-serve gourmet coffee.

This room was oceanfront and it was on the fourteenth floor.

Randall had cracked the sliding glass door and the waves crashing against the shore outside made for remarkable music. Simone stood in place and listened for a while.

Randall never disturbed much in the room. He even made his own bed most times. But sometimes Simone would beat him to it, be there just after he awakened and do it herself.

He didn't move much when he slept. Simone assumed that was from the peace of having somewhere safe and clean to lay your head. People tended to take that for granted.

Tonight his discarded clothes were in a heap on the floor, so Simone bent to pick them up for washing so he'd have something clean for in the morning, but as she reached down, the bathroom door opened, and Randall was there.

She hadn't even heard the shower turn off.

He was standing there, wearing nothing but drops of water on his toffee-toned skin.

Beneath his normal layers of clothes, Simone never would have guessed Randall was camouflaging such a nice build. His arms were toned, his legs thick and muscular. His chest was strong, solid and bare.

Simone liked a bare chest on a man.

And…his…

Cock.

It hung there, lovely and lengthy.

Simone thought at least Randall would place his hand *there*, attempt to cover at least *that* part of him. But he didn't. He just stood there in the door of the bathroom and stared at her.

Mouth agape, Simone stammered for words.

"I was just…I'm…uh, I'm sorry, Randall. I was just bringing towels and grabbing your clothes."

But Randall threw up his hand.

"You're fine," he said. And he took a seat.

He went on to make mention of the weather or some other odd thing. In the chair next to the wall, naked, Randall was talking to Simone as if he were fully clothed.

Simone reminded herself to keep her eyes on Randall's face, not on his bare chest and arms, but especially not on his…

His cock stood between his legs like a trophy, dancing back and forth, forth and back. Randall talked as if he didn't notice.

When Simone simply couldn't take it anymore, she handed him a towel from the folded stack in her arms.

He looked at it strangely, squinting his hazel eyes, then with sudden realization, he draped it over his lap.

"Sorry," Randall said softly.

And Simone said, "No need to apologize. You were comfortable. I'm glad you can be that comfortable with me."

"But you're not that comfortable with me," Randall said.

"I am," Simone answered, "but I think we have different views on comfort. I'm not an exhibitionist."

"Nor am I."

Simone was suddenly afraid she had offended Randall, and

she hadn't wanted to do that. More embarrassed now than when she had walked in, Simone got up and walked toward the door.

"I'll let you get some rest now."

"Okay."

But his voice was closer than it had been. Randall was behind her, walking her to the door.

"If you never knew me, never saw me the way you see me, you'd never know. But just *so* you know, Simone, I know how to love a woman."

"I never said..."

"I know, I know," Randall interrupted. "I just think it needed to be said, that I'm more than what you see here. I was different, once. I had a job. I had a home."

Simone nodded.

And then there were Randall's hands, easing up from behind. He placed a palm on each breast.

Simone breathed in, then out.

"I even had a woman or two. Once I had one who was all about me playing with her tits. She'd walk around topless just to get me going."

And Randall was getting Simone going with his words, with his slow and steady rubbing of his hands over her breasts and nipples. With one hand, he reached behind the open button of her blouse and found the lacy fabric of her bra. He slipped inside, so that his hand was on her skin.

"She didn't care if I never made it anywhere else," Randall continued. "And she had the most sensitive nipples. They rose and they were hard before my fingers or my lips even touched them. Like yours are now, Simone."

Simone could only nod.

"But I'm not a breast man," Randall said. "Care to guess what kind of man I am, Simone?"

Simone shook her head.

"Fair enough," he said. "I had a woman once who was all about the hot spots. It was foreplay or no play. She really taught me how to love like a man."

Randall's hands moved from Simone's breasts to her shoulders, where he initiated a mini massage. Then he brushed a hand across the back of her neck.

Stepping closer, he flicked his tongue against the back of her ear.

Simone wished she could see him now. Wished she could turn around and open her mouth, have Randall force his tongue inside. She wanted to have him pressed against her so that she could find some sort of relief, but Randall only continued slowly, touching places that sent waves and vibrations throughout her body, places that hadn't been touched in months, places she would have never guessed would turn her on...between her shoulder blades, circling around her navel, dropping to his knees to kiss the backs of her knees.

Randall was speaking again, his voice as low and steady as a well-oiled motor.

"That stuff, that's all fine and good, but that's not what really gets me off."

Simone wondered if he would allow her to do something to him, if maybe he would let her return the favor, maybe fall to her knees, snatch the towel away and take him in her mouth.

But it would appear that Randall wouldn't.

Instead, he lifted Simone's skirt, hiking it roughly until it rested in folds and wrinkles around her waist.

But he didn't turn her around. He wouldn't let her see. Randall was close enough now that Simone felt his cock against her ass.

He was hard and he was big. She hadn't been expecting that

before tonight, and she was hardly ever wrong about people.

Simone heard the air conditioner kick on in the background at about the same time that she felt Randall's fingers wedging between the cheeks of her ass.

Simone's mouth fell open in a silent gasp.

He was doing just what she'd thought and hoped he might.

Randall rubbed first, and Simone pressed against his finger, ready but unwilling to appear eager. And when she was just loose enough, he gave her his index finger.

Her anus clutched tightly around his finger, but Randall managed his way in and out, out and in. He continued this ass play for what seemed like hours, and in a second, his fingers were gone.

"I like swimming," Randall said then, inserting a finger in then out of her cunt. "That's my thing. And as wet as you are, I'm gonna have to keep myself from drowning."

Randall entered her. The *swish swish* of Simone's wetness echoed in the darkened room. Randall filled Simone with every solid inch of him. She was sure she felt him at the base of her belly. She forced her knees apart to be as open as she could, taking all of him in.

"You know, Simone, I'm a simple man," Randall said. "I don't need a fancy backstroke. And I like taking my time getting to the edge."

Simone was at the edge. She clutched the fibers of the carpet. She dropped her forehead to the floor.

Randall pulled her by her hips into him as he gave her stroke after stroke, some long, some short, some quick, some slow, all an endless stream of beautiful friction that filled Simone with ecstasy.

"Ummm." It came through gritted teeth and tight lips. She hadn't wanted him to know. "Ummm," Simone said.

"That's right," Randall said. "You come first."

And Simone came, pushing back against Randall's cock, the *swish swish* louder when she released what had been building inside her.

Her arms trembled beneath her own weight, weakened at her release.

Simone struggled not to collapse as Randall pumped harder and faster until he himself was coming.

His growl was that of a tiger's, and Simone was a cub, crying and sighing beneath him.

She could have slept this way, easy. She could have lain with him on the floor and let her eyes flutter closed. But Henry would be wondering where she was, and she didn't want to blow Randall's cover.

She said, "I have to go, Randall."

And Randall nodded, his chin against her back.

"But you'll come again." He said it instead of asking and Simone was okay with that.

She said, "Yes, Randall, I will."

DIRTY WHITE ENVELOPE

Ellie Vokes

It took me three years to tell Ron I wanted to be treated like a whore.

"A what?" he said. He ran his hands through his long brown hair.

"Well, not all the time, of course. Just for one night. Maybe a couple of hours. I'm not even sure what the appeal is, but I've always had this fantasy of wearing a slutty hooker getup and then going to a cheap motel and being treated like a whore."

He stared at me for several long minutes. "Okay. But just how far do you want to take this? What're your limits?"

"I want the whole experience. Pick me up beside the road. Take me to a cheap motel. Talk trash to me. I trust you, babe. Just use your imagination. And if I don't like something, I'll use our safeword, red, and we'll talk about what's going on."

"All right, all right." Ideas were brewing in his head. "But only if I can play a role, too."

"What would that be?"

"You'll find out soon enough."

* * *

Two days later I was dressed in fishnet stockings, a mini jean skirt, tank top and heels, standing in front of a few bars in downtown feeling debased and humiliated. People stared. Two college jocks muttered something under their breath and then laughed hysterically. A woman held her purse closer to her body. I never wanted to be rescued so badly in my life.

Ron pulled up in his Ford Escort a few minutes later. He rolled down his window. I walked over, bent down, my blonde hair falling inside the car, and stuck my head in the window. I loved what I saw. He was wearing a priest outfit.

His hair was tied back into a neat ponytail. Tanned skin hugged a white plastic collar. A gold cross hung around his neck. He was dressed in black.

"Hello, Father. You need some company tonight?"

"Hop in."

"Thanks, it was getting cold out there. You got someplace we can go?"

"Yeah. The Motel Six is down the road here. You been busy tonight?" He put his hand on my thigh. "What do you mostly do? Blow jobs? Sex? Anal?"

"Money talks, Father." He pulled into a Motel 6. "Wait here." He went inside and paid for the room. Ron looked cheesy in his priest outfit. I wondered how many fake priests paid for a room at the Motel 6. I was pleased he was really getting into this.

He came back out, keys in his hands. "We have the room till eleven a.m."

"Ron, you're breaking character. Don't do that."

"Sorry, babe," he said, changing the subject. "I never got your name."

"Bridget."

"Well, Bridget, here's our room."

Never before had I seen such a cheap room. Bedspreads exploded in primary colors. Water stains decorated the walls. Stale cigarette smoke lingered. I didn't even want to check out the bathroom.

If Ron was grossed out, he didn't show it. He sat on the bed and pulled out a white envelope. "Is this enough for whatever I want to do to you?" It contained five crisp twenty-dollar bills.

"Wow, that is quite a bit of money, but I need to know exactly what you're looking for, Father."

"Oral, straight sex, and I want to talk real dirty to you."

"Sounds like you'll be saying a lot of Hail Marys tomorrow."

"You're the real sinner, whore." He grabbed my hair. "You've been out in front of that bar all night, with how many men? And how many times have you had to clean your mouth and cunt of come?"

I was taken aback. It was more than I could have asked for. I was ready to come just from those words alone.

Ron's pants were tight against his hard cock. I reached for his zipper, exposing his cock. "Go fill that bucket with water and wash my feet."

Warm water filled the cream-colored plastic basin. I knelt before Ron and laid a white terry-cloth towel beneath his feet. Multicolored stains spotted the taupe carpet. Gently, I massaged and washed his feet, getting each crevice between his toes.

"That's nice. Very good." He caressed my hair. "Tell me, Bridget, what is your job?"

"To please you, Father. My only job is to please you."

"Yes, that is correct. It would please me very much if you worshipped my feet."

I kissed his big toe, putting it in my mouth, running my tongue in and around all his toes. My warm tongue licked the entire length of his foot and up his calf. He shuddered.

"Come here. I want to feel your stockings."

His hands were rough from working in construction all day. They roamed over the netting of my stockings, catching on the nylon. Cheap seams ran up the backs of my legs. The gold cross dangled from his neck as he reached for my breasts. His cock waved in my face. He took it and slapped it across my face twice, then put his balls in my mouth.

"I'm not sure if you can be saved. Suck them." His balls were taut and full in my mouth. Sucking on them, I reached up to jerk him off.

I took his cock in my mouth, choking on his thick bulbous head. Spit dripped down my chest. He held me against his belly, fucking my throat.

"That's a good whore," he said.

He opened the nightstand drawer and took out the Holy Bible.

"Stand up and turn around."

My jean skirt exposed the top of the fishnet panty hose and showed I wasn't wearing any panties. He sighed in approval, grabbed my ass and bent me over.

"Naughty girls need punishment." He spanked me lightly with the Bible several times. I feigned cries of pain. "You must repent."

He stood back up, towering over me. "Father, if it would please you, please touch my pussy."

His thick fingers delighted in masturbating me through the nylon fabric. Wetness dripped down my leg. Precome oozed from his engorged crimson head. He pushed me onto the bed and tore the crotch of my hose.

"I can taste them. The others. I need to clean you before I stick my cock in you." He took his tongue and ran it along my slit several times.

"Don't stop. Please, Father. Please keep doing it."

"No. I want you to fuck me now that I have you clean."

He sat back on the bed, black shirt still on and the white collar snug around his neck. I didn't want him to take it off. I removed my top, exposing my tits, and took off my jean skirt but left my hose and heels on.

"See that envelope over there? You don't get to take that money unless you atone for your sins. I'm the one you need to impress. And I don't even want to look at you when you fuck me."

"Yes, Father."

I mounted him, reverse-cowgirl style. I let his cock play with my clit while he talked dirty for a bit more.

"You should be so lucky that I picked you up in front of that dump." He grabbed my blonde hair, pulling my head back, whispering in my ear, "You have the closest thing to God's cock inside you, whore." I moved faster against his cock, my slit engorged with fluid. He slipped inside me, his balls flush against the folds of my skin. We both let out a moan.

"Father, you do feel amazing. You were truly blessed when God made you."

His hands played with my clit as I rode his cock faster. My tits bounced, nipples hard and flushed. His breath hot on my neck. Mixed smells from the room made me dizzy with delight. I felt cheap.

"I'm going to come inside you. Fill you with God's seed. Ask me permission before you come."

"Yes, Father."

He took over, pumping inside me. Grunting and moaning. Our neighbors banged on the wall for us to be quiet as the cheap headboard banged against the wall. We ignored them.

"Father, may I come?"

"Yes, you may."

My pussy twitched and quivered around his thick dick.

"You whore," he said.

All I could do was scream, "Yes." It was everything I wanted. He came inside me as promised. When he finished I got off of him and watched his come dribble out of me. I cleaned it off my leg and disposed of it down my throat, washing away our sins.

We cuddled on the brightly colored bedspread.

"What did you think?" he asked.

"I thought it was great. But why a priest?"

"I always wanted to do a role-playing situation where I could be a priest gone bad and I thought this would be a great situation to enact that. Was it okay?"

"Yeah, it was great. I'm really glad you decided to do that. It made the experience so much better for me. What did you think?"

"I enjoyed it. We should do something like this again."

"Oh, we will."

We didn't stay until morning. The room was just too disgusting. I got home and took a long shower in my very clean home that didn't smell. I haven't been back to the Motel 6 since.

TAILGATING AT THE CEDAR INN

Delilah Devlin

I stepped out of the shower onto chipped and cracked aqua-blue tiles with grout so dingy it was hard to tell what color it had been. Not that the bathroom was dirty, thank god. Just old. Like the rest of the '60s-built motels I'd found on the little back-country road.

I toweled my hair, then shook my head like a dog, not caring where the droplets landed. It wasn't a mess I'd have to clean up. For one last night I could be irresponsible, messy, even if it was only in a small way.

I draped the towel over the edge of the old white tub and sauntered naked into the small room with the double bed. It smelled of tobacco and industrial cleansers. The bedding looked clean, if a little nappy from wear, but I peeled back the quilt-top and tossed it on the floor anyway. Pristine white sheets beckoned.

Just as I lay back, sighing with relief, sounds from outside the room jarred me from my happy haze. Tires squealed, masculine laughter bellowed through the thin walls and car doors slammed.

I sighed and stared at the bared rafters above me. The laughter faded. I reached across to flip off the switch to the nightstand lamp with its yellowed shade. Lying in the darkness, I willed my body to relax, one limb at a time. I'd driven three hundred miles that day. I'd have gone another fifty for a decent hotel, but the shorter route my Garmin had found led me through narrow two-lane roads deep in the Ozark Mountains. I doubted I'd have found anything nicer.

I should have stuck to the Interstate, but I'd wanted to shave some miles. Little did I know that the route would keep my foot busy pushing on the gas pedal then the brake the whole way. Exhausted, nerves shattered, I'd seen the crooked vacancy sign outside the Cedar Inn and made my decision on the spot, swerving into the empty gravel parking lot. Not until I'd opened the door to my tiny, musty room did I have second thoughts about my decision. But how bad could it really be? I'd turned on the swamp cooler set into a window frame and felt my hair frizz instantly.

Not that I'd really cared. There wasn't anyone around to impress. Other than the clerk at the front desk, a skinny, twenty-something redneck with puppy-dog eyes, the place was deserted. I'd shivered a little bit at the thought, double-bolted my room door and checked the locks on the remaining window. Visions of the shower scene from *Psycho* didn't put me off taking a long, lukewarm soak to wash away the road grime and sweat.

The cooler purred, spilling muggy air into the room. The sheets felt clammy. Still, I grew calm as my body warmed the sheets beneath me, then a little horny when I wondered if the room might have little peepholes for the clerk to watch me. He'd been cute if a little skinny. I wouldn't mind if he watched—at least not in my fantasies. Who knew how long it would be until I felt comfortable enough, private enough to indulge in a little one-handed play once I'd reached my destination and my grandmother slept in the room next to me.

I slipped a hand between my thighs and lazily trailed my fingers through my cleft until my breath caught and heat pooled. I raised my knees and let them fall open, tilted my hips and thrust two fingers inside my pussy. I wasn't in a hurry. I wasn't even that eager to come. The motion soothed and excited, allowing my mind to let go of my troubles—the firing, the break-up, the move to my grandmother's house—and focus only on the pleasure curling deep inside my core.

When the blare of a TV sounded from outside, I had third and fourth thoughts about my decision to stop here for the night. *What the hell?* Why had someone moved their television set outside rather than watch in the seclusion of his room where the sound would be muffled somewhat?

I gritted my teeth, swung my legs over the side of the bed and reached for shorts and a tee, slipping them over my nude body and the keys in my pocket before I stomped to the door and flung it open.

Not that the two men sitting on the truck noticed me—at first.

Under the single floodlight that illuminated the parking lot, I noted the construction company logo on the side of the pickup backed up to the door of the room beside mine. Then I eyed the large men seated on the sides of the truck bed, their shirts gone, faded jeans stretched over thick thighs. Their attention was glued to the basketball game blaring from the small screen of the TV they had set in the bed of the truck on top of a white ice chest. They held Budweisers in their grips.

At last, one of the men's heads turned. He spotted me then

whistled at his friend. Soon both their gazes peered down.

I felt foolish standing in my bare feet with my wet hair spiked around my head. Why hadn't I simply put a pillow over my head to muffle their noise? But I was testy. Moody. I'd lost my job, had a blow-up with my boyfriend over the fact I wouldn't be splitting rent with him for a while, and cut my nose off to spite my own face by breaking up with him. Homeless now, I had no options. Grandma's in Little Rock was my last resort.

Tonight would be my last night of freedom before I moved under her roof and abided by her rules. She'd pay the bills—*if* I knuckled under and went back to school. Something I resented after being on my own for a couple of years, living by my rules.

Which might have been exactly why I remained, rooted to that spot. The men seated on the truck would never meet Grandma's high standards.

Sweat gleamed on their naked chests and both of them were thickly muscled and a little dirty—as though they'd come straight from work without the benefit of a shower.

The shine only served to emphasize the depth of the musculature and their starkly masculine features. Their tanned, leathery skin stretched across cheeks and jaws that were sharpened to rough edges by hard work.

Both their gazes homed on me, and while I knew the smart thing would have been to retreat without a word to my room and relock the door, I tilted my chin and thrust out my chest. "Can't you watch the game in your room?"

"We botherin' you, sweetheart?" the one closest to me said, sliding off the truck to land in front of me.

I peered a long way up and frowned into the face tilted my way. We stood close enough I could see the bristles of his evening shadow. He wore a ball cap that shadowed his eyes, but glints of blond hair shone beneath it. "It's late. I was trying to sleep."

"It's not that late," he drawled. "Join us for a beer?"

I glanced behind him and noted the grin on his buddy's face. He was bare-headed with shaggy brown hair and a devilish quirk to his firm lips. The game seemed to have lost its fascination. Their gazes drank me down like I was a long, cool drink.

I barely resisted the urge to jut my hip and twirl my hair.

"Bobby, the night clerk, can vouch for us if you're wonderin' whether we're safe," the one beside me said, amusement lingering in his husky voice.

I shouldn't have been tempted. However, my body still hummed pleasurably from the heat I'd drawn with my own lazy fingers. Even sweaty, the two men were tempting. Both young, in good shape. Both interested if their sharpening gazes were any indication.

And what the hell? It wasn't as if I had anyone to answer to. Not at this moment. There was no boyfriend to betray.

My mouth went dry and I swallowed. "Is the beer cold?"

His friend bent and picked up the TV, setting it to the side to open the top of the cooler. The can of beer he drew out was wet with nuggets of ice sliding off the sides. He flicked open the top and handed it me. "Like basketball?"

"Not particularly."

His head canted. "Not from around here, are you?"

"I'm from Iowa."

"A corn-fed girl," he murmured, his gaze dropping to my chest.

"Not a cow or a pig," I ground out.

"Don't put words in my mouth." His lips twitched then stretched into a lazy grin. "Name's Owen. My buddy here's Chris."

I gave them both a narrow-eyed look, then turned and hopped up to sit on the open tailgate. "I'm Kelsey," I said, pretending to be more confident than I really was.

The TV fell silent. The man in the truck bed eased down beside me. The other one stood in front of me, feet braced apart as he took another draw on his beer. "Where ya headed?" he asked after crushing the can in his hand and tossing it behind me to land with a thud on the truck bed.

"Little Rock."

Chris grunted. Beside me, Owen chuckled. "Small world."

"I take it that's where you're from?"

"Yep. Visitin' family?"

"My grandmother. I'm moving there to help out."

"It's nice you're able to do for her."

More like she was doing for me, but I wasn't willing to admit just how stupid I'd been. Lowering my head, I said, "We're helping each other out." My expression must have fallen because Chris stepped closer and tucked a finger under my chin to raise my face.

I didn't bat his hand away as I should have, but met his steady gaze. I don't know what he saw, but his lips relaxed into a semblance of a smile.

The slight motion drew my attention, and I realized for the first time just how attractive that mouth was. His lips were full, and when they stretched, white teeth flashed. A man with good teeth. Something I imagined wasn't plentiful in backwoods Arkansas.

I stared a moment too long. Heat crept slowly down my neck and across my chest. My nipples tightened, poking at the thin tee stretched across my breasts. He didn't miss the sudden surge of arousal because his feet shuffled closer.

Breathing became something I had to think about doing. I swept my upper lip with my tongue, opening my mouth to say something, but he bent toward me. Slowly. His narrowed eyes daring me to draw away.

I didn't. The beer was plucked from my lifeless fingers and I gripped the edge of the tailgate, wrapping them around it to brace myself for a kiss.

His mouth was tentative, teasing, sliding over mine and rubbing in a circular movement that pulled me with it, until I was moving with him, following to make sure I didn't lose the seductive heat.

When he drew back, he smiled. "You know, sweetheart, you don't have to be alone tonight."

I blinked and glanced to the side at Owen.

"Package deal," Chris said, drawing my attention back.

Package deal. Two packages. Mine to enjoy.

I opened my mouth and drew a quick breath, suddenly nervous. "I don't..." I cleared my throat. "I've never..."

"We have," he said quickly, cupping my chin and sliding a thumb over my still moist lower lip. "Nothin' to be worried about. Cedar Inn's quiet. Clean. You've got the single room, right? Come to ours, and we'll shove the mattresses together. Plenty of room."

Moisture seeped to soak the crotch of my panties. My clit throbbed and hardened. I could end it now and go back to my bed, slide my fingers over the knot and come in an instant, but their scent and heat surrounded me. I imagined being sandwiched between them both—slick, hot skin sliding against mine, front and back. I squeezed my thighs because they were beginning to quiver. Suddenly, I had options. One safe. One not so much—but wickedly enticing.

"No pressure," Owen said, dropping a slow kiss on the corner of my shoulder. "You call the shots. Whatever you want."

What I wanted was for them to make a move. Make up my mind for me, because I didn't think I was capable of speaking.

Chris laid his palms on the tops of my bare thighs and slid his thumbs between them, then slowly opened me, stepping closer, forcing me wider again until his crotch was flush with mine.

His erection was impossible to ignore. A thick, insistent bulge. "Maybe you don't want a bed?" he murmured. "Maybe you want it here?"

His crudeness excited me. Challenged me in a way I'd never have accepted in my former life. I tossed my head. "But someone will see."

"Maybe. Might only be Bobby, but he won't mind. Will you?"

Owen slipped a hand behind me and rucked up my shirt until the fabric bunched under my arms. My belly bare, the warm night air blew across my skin, feeling like a caress. My belly tightened.

I glanced between them, noted the tension riding both their jaws. They wouldn't make a move without my consent, but they'd pounce the second I did. I let the moment stretch.

Then I leaned forward and raised my arms, keeping my gaze locked with Chris's as Owen pulled the garment all the way off.

Both men breathed deeply as they stared at my breasts. Chris cupped one, hefted it in his palm then squeezed. Owen wet a finger and circled the other nipple, pausing to scratch a nail across the tip. It hardened.

"You're pretty," Chris muttered.

"Doesn't sound like you're happy about that."

"Don't pay any mind to what he says," Owen said. "He's hard. He doesn't think straight when he gets that way. Take it as a compliment."

Chris plucked my nipple and released it, watching it bounce back. His gaze darted to mine again, then he slipped his fingers inside the waist of my shorts and rubbed the top of my mound. "Can I take these off, too?"

I didn't mind his blunt tone this time. The air between us felt charged with a current that pricked my nipples and caused my pussy to contract.

In for a penny... I was already committed. So hot I was panting. I nodded, then gasped when Owen eased me back and Chris went to work unsnapping my shorts and dragging them off my legs.

Then Owen pushed me forward and slid behind me, urging me to rest against his naked chest. Chris opened his jeans and pushed them off his hips, freeing his cock. He leaned over me, pressing me harder against Owen who chuckled as Chris hooked his elbows beneath my thighs and lifted my bottom.

"A condom?" I gasped, one last shred of sanity remaining before my mind completely filled with the sight of him. He was thick, long, a straight cudgel of a cock. Twice the girth of the last man I'd had.

"Pocket," he ground out.

I reached for the scrunched-up top of his jeans and pulled out his wallet. My hands shook, but I found the trifold of foil packets and tore one off. He watched as I clumsily cloaked him in the latex sheath. Then he was there, pushing inside me.

The moment he entered me, my mind clicked. *Fuck, I was really doing this.* Really taking on a stranger while his friend held me, his hands cupping my breasts and his cock grinding against my backside through his jeans.

And I wanted him nude as well. Wanted them both rutting, both sinking deep.

I wriggled inside Owen's embrace.

Chris shook his head, his nostrils flared. "Want me to stop?" he bit out.

"Fuck no. Owen?"

Owen laughed. The sound edgy, taut.

Chris urged my legs around his back and stood, lifting me from the truck bed. Behind me, I heard the rustle of clothing, the snap of latex. I didn't look back and instead nuzzled into Chris's shoulder to hide my face. I should be ashamed. But instead, I was grinning, and then nipping his skin, causing him to groan and thrust.

I didn't know how they would manage it, but trusted that they knew a way.

"Ready."

Chris nodded, then turned and sat on the tailgate, leaning back and bringing me with him. Behind me, hands cupped my ass, pulled my cheeks apart. I moaned in protest, and Owen's thumbs slipped farther down, tucking into my pussy, sliding along Chris's dick, then stretching upward to make a space.

"No way," I muttered.

"There's room. I promise," Owen said, a trace of humor in his strained voice. Then he was pushing inside me, forcing his way atop Chris's thick cock.

"Fuck, it's tight." Chris said, gasping.

"I'll move for us both," Owen whispered and gave a tentative stroke, then another, deepening his thrusts as he squeezed his way inside me.

Chris leaned back a little farther on the truck, then placed my knees on either side of his hips. I bent over him, scooping at his mouth while Owen pleasured us both with his short, sharp strokes.

I'd never been so full or stretched. Friction built. I'd be sore in the morning, but I didn't care, gritting my teeth to hold out for just a few seconds more. My channel flooded with moisture, oozing around the two cocks. They both moved inside me, one pushing, one pulling. A finger breached my ass, plunging deep.

I howled, bucking atop Chris, wriggling my ass to encourage

Owen to power harder. Sweat slicked my belly and my back and rolled off my chin.

Chris cupped my breast, twisted my nipple, released it, then finally pinched it hard.

I came with a yelp, grinding down on his cock as he rolled his belly to force his cock deeper and held still while Owen jerked hard inside me. Then I moaned, long and loud, collapsing against Chris's chest until Owen jerked again and then settled against me, his hot breaths gusting in my ear.

"Think we might make it to that bed, now?" Owen gasped.

I laughed. "Still got legs? I don't."

The three of us chuckled. Hands smoothed over my back and ass, my belly. Owen pulled away. Chris came up on his arms and slid to the edge of the tailgate. "Hold on." He walked with me wrapped around him to my door.

"Key," I muttered. "Pocket."

"Got it," Owen said. He fumbled with the lock and pushed inside. The bed, with its covers turned down, beckoned. Chris knelt on the edge then came down on top of me. This was when I realized he was still hard as a post inside me.

"I gotta move," he growled.

I grinned. "Bet you do."

His grunt was all male. "You're a sassy thing."

"Who says that?"

"You're not in Iowa anymore."

"All you Arkansas boys this horny?"

His grin was a tight flash. He pushed my legs off his waist and shoved my thighs toward my chest. One large hand cupped my ass, cradling me, while he braced his weight on the other arm and began to thrust. *Hard.* His eyes narrowed, his chest expanded with the effort, his muscles rippling with the effort as he plowed into me.

I didn't mind, even scrunched so tight I could barely breathe. Watching his face tighten, his lips draw away from his teeth as he drew near, I wondered how I'd ever been satisfied before with a man who didn't like sweat or effort and whose lazy lovemaking had only managed to warm me. Sure, Derek had gotten me off, *eventually*, but he hadn't been this powerful. This physical.

Chris thrust hard and held. His head thrust back, and he groaned. I felt him tremble inside me, felt the gush through the latex. He lowered my butt, and I stretched out my legs on either side him while he slowly rocked against me, both of us savoring the sensation of him moving in my liquid heat.

We rested like that, me still pinned to the bed with Owen lying on his side beside us, a wide grin splitting his mouth.

When Chris stirred, he gave a deep rumbling groan. "Still need to sleep?"

"What about your game?"

"I've got a game," Owen said, his tone sly.

Chris and I both turned to stare at Owen who gave a casual shrug—completely at odds with the tension causing his cock to stiffen against his belly. "Depends on how flexible you are, Kelsey. And whether you're any good at...multitasking."

I don't know what made me laugh so hard—the fact he'd actually used the word "multitasking" with his thick Southern drawl or the shot of adrenaline that spiked my blood. However, when I quieted, I let him drape me sideways on the bed, my head hanging over the edge for Chris to take my mouth while Owen knelt, my thighs draped over his shoulders for him to prove to me just how diligent a country boy could be.

I drifted in a happy sensual haze. This was so much better than the lazy orgasm I'd been willing to settle for. A brilliant send-off to the next chapter of my life. Rather than entering it with my shoulders drooping with disappointment, I felt sure the rosy blush of excitement would linger for a long time—a secret I'd keep to myself and savor for its delicious naughtiness.

Owen slid a tongue between my folds and lapped like a dog from just beneath my pussy to my clit. My heels dug into his back.

Chris leaned over me, his dick down my throat, his body braced on his arms as he moved in smooth shallow motions across my tongue to the back of my throat.

I felt like one of those blow-up dolls, not expected to do anything but provide a convenient hole or two for the two men to use. Not that I really minded. Lying helpless, feeling overwhelmed by all the testosterone and male musk stinking up the room. I was really quite content.

I knew with feminine surety that we'd be fucking until dawn. When I rolled out of the parking lot, I'd ache from head to toe and would have some bruises in intimate places. I also knew that even though I'd give them a casual good-bye, I'd find a way to slip my cell phone number into one of their pockets. Not that I expected this to develop into something more than what it really was.

I might have begun this trip thinking the life I entered was a last resort, but I had options. Two of them at the moment. I reached around Chris's buttocks and slid a finger between his cheeks.

"God damn," he whispered.

My mouth stretched as I smiled around his cock. Yeah, I wasn't in Iowa anymore.

STILETTO'S BIG SCORE

Michael A. Gonzales

Excited by life, cinema and men, forty-five-year-old former blaxploitation icon Miki Jamison glanced at her smooth cinnamon-hued face in the movie-trailer bathroom mirror and remembered when she was still a young B-movie actress trying to make her way in Hollywood without playing maids or whores.

Of course, while the ever-rotating planet had changed the world plenty in those two decades since her career fizzled and flopped after a few movies, Miki was glad she'd agreed to make the comeback film *Savage Holiday*. It was the smartest decision she had made in years, and Miki had no problem reviving her 1975 part as female action hero and custom shoe designer, Sharon Stiletto.

In addition, she dug working with the energetic director Alex Reid. As the auteur behind two critically acclaimed, post-Tarantino crime flicks with lots of witty dialogue and graphic violence, Alex was brilliant, though sometimes he ranted like a coked-out madman.

After shooting their first flashback scene that Monday morning, Miki returned to her deluxe trailer parked in front of Cortes's Bar on 125th Street and St. Nicolas Avenue. Sitting on the small bed, she took off her high heels and flung them across the room. Silently massaging her sore feet, she wished she could just grab her fine costar and head back to her suite at the Sutton Hotel.

Located on 110th and Fifth Avenue, the Sutton was the first five-star hotel in Harlem. A fifty-story sky palace, it was designed by Blake Parks, a premier architect in the nineties who was once a mentor to Frank Gehry. While some of the less refined tastes of the community thought the towering building was nothing more than an eyesore of twisted titanium and sparkling glass, architectural writers raved that the Sutton was a breakthrough in postmodernism.

"Stimulating, beautiful and full of light," wrote the *New York Times* critic. "From wherever one stands in the changing community, all one has to do is look up to see the gleaming metal and glass building." Truthfully, like the exterior of the few Parks structures Miki had seen in her adopted hometown of San Francisco, it was in her opinion one of the ugliest buildings she had ever seen, but at least her suite was stunning.

However, instead of lounging on the bedroom terrace catching an autumnal penthouse breeze or standing in the plush living room pouring another glass of champagne, Miki was working in the heart of the hood.

Dressed to impress in a red and black flowing Pucci maxidress for the flashback scenes, she had worn a similar outfit in her 1975 magnum opus *Foxy Stiletto*. Flashing her full breasts to the world, the movie had transformed Miki Jamison from a nice New York City girl into a ripe sex symbol.

A generation of young boys had flocked to the theater back

when Pam Grier, Tamara Dobson and Miki Jamison were kicking ass with sass; for many of those fans she became the first object of their adolescent desire. With her perfect Afro that was sexy and seductive, she rolled around naked in their wet dreams as her hairy snatch and hardened nipples caused many sticky pajama bottoms come morning.

Yet for the last twenty years, she had lived like a normal person, owning a string of beauty shops in the Bay Area and staying out of the limelight. Married briefly in the eighties, she was divorced and childless and had somehow managed, despite her drinking, to look ten years younger than her age.

By some strange pop-culture circumstances a few years before, her name began popping up in random places and fame rediscovered her by accident. "Who is Miki Jamison?" a contestant answered correctly on "Jeopardy!" one night as the real Miki finished her Lean Cuisine.

Days after the "Jeopardy!" name-drop, an *Entertainment Weekly* reporter wrote a profile on Jamison's brief career, calling her "the Bettie Page of blaxploitation." Smiling to herself as she read the article, Miki recalled her once-upon-a-time, crazy Hollywood years.

A few weeks later, wunderkind director Alex Reid tracked her down and invited Miki to lunch in hopes of begging her to come out of retirement.

With him dressed in a vintage pin-striped suit that gave him the aura of a Runyon character, they ate at the Chateau Marmont. "You were the godmother of them all," Reid declared; spittle sprayed when he talked. "Coffy, Cleopatra Jones, you were the best." Fattening her ego with champagne and compliments, he spoke passionately about her old grindhouse reels.

With a beaming grin that would shame the Cheshire cat, one would have thought the hyperactive director was about to have a heart attack. "None of them bitches had what Stiletto had. You were the shit with a capital S."

"You were a fan, huh?" Miki coyly asked.

"A fan? The way you used to pull out your blade and say, 'Don't make me slice ya, baby.' Fuck a fan, I was in love."

After revealing the inner fan boy beneath his Hollywood snark, Reid snapped his fingers at a passing waitress and ordered two bottles of champagne. "Don't take this the wrong way," he stage-whispered, dramatically leaning across the table, "but I wanted to be you. I wanted to be the bad Black chick that sliced first and asked questions later. I wanted to be that ebony bombshell with bazooka breasts and dynamite in her kisses. I mean, who wouldn't want to be a six-foot-tall, bad mamma jamma with sharp knives and an attitude?

"And don't even let me get started on the shoes. Stiletto heels, damn. I went from puppy love to full-fledged foot fetish after seeing those heels. That's why I feel obligated to make *Savage Holiday* as my own Stiletto movie. Let's just say it'll be one white boy's way of giving back to the cinematic soul sisters who raised me."

Swayed by the director's passion, a million-dollar paycheck and the best script she'd read in years, Miki signed on the dotted line. Although she thought things couldn't get any more perfect, when Reid told her that Lockhart Williams had agreed to play the notorious drug dealer King Johnson, they did.

Back when Miki Jamison was still a young actress working in American International Pictures, making movies like *Prison Sisters* (1972), *Beige Bomber* (1973), *Baby Go-Go* (1974) and her most famous film, *Foxy Stiletto* (1975), she had sworn never to fuck her costars. Especially pretty boys with names like Billy Dee or Roundtree, dudes who dressed like pimps and thought their non-stinkable shit was precious as gold. With their egos the size of stadiums, it was easy to avoid the obvious train wrecks and overly macho former football players known for putting their broads in the hospital.

However, shining star Lockhart Williams, with his hazel eyes and solid build, was the exception to the rule. Indeed, since Miki first saw him playing a Black Panther in the film *Prophets of Rage* (1972) opposite Ron O'Neal as Huey Newton, the man caused her clit to twitch.

Standing over six feet, he was the first contemporary actor she ever had a serious crush on. Like a cocoa version of Burt Reynolds, Williams was playful and tough and had an onscreen persona that was cool as ice.

A Shakespearean-trained actor forced to do B-movies to survive in Hollywood, he and Miki had met once at the Playboy mansion years ago. After an hour of heavy conversation, Williams excused himself from the room and Miki never saw him in person again.

On that October afternoon, the entire production of *Savage Holiday* checked into the glam Sutton Hotel. Miki soon fell in love with the black and green Italian marble walls inside the bathroom. Standing under the soothing warm water of the shower, she lathered herself with L'Occitane body gel, washing away the grit of her five-hour flight to LaGuardia Airport.

Twenty minutes later, stepping out of the tub that was deep enough to swim in, Miki dried herself thoroughly, lotioned her body and slipped on one of the thick bathrobes hanging on the back of the door. After combing and styling her long, kinky hair, she put on a pair of high-heeled mules and walked across the lush beige carpet to the kitchen. Opening the refrigerator, Miki popped the cork on one of the bottles of Veuve Clicquot stocked on the bottom shelf.

Standing in front of the panoramic window view of Central Park, she gulped her champagne while admiring the changing leaves on the trees. After so many years away from the city of her birth, Miki loved being in New York in the fall.

The sudden ringing of the doorbell startled her. "Delivery," a thirtysomething Black man stuttered, obviously recognizing her from the movies of his youth. Sometimes when guys met their old jerk-off/pinup material in the flesh, they were flustered.

Rolling a fancy platinum cart containing a few wardrobe bags and shoeboxes, the hotel staffer walked into the massive suite, opened the closet and hung them up. There was also a manila envelope on the cart that he handed to her.

"Thank you very much," she said, giving him a ten-dollar tip. She learned long ago that if you treated the hotel staff well, they looked out for you.

"No problem, Miss Jamison." The bellhop pushed the cart back outside. "If you need anything, just ask." Minutes later, she opened the envelope, pulling out a CD and a folded letter.

Scribbled on nice hotel stationery was a note from her director. *I trust you're happy with your suite. In the wardrobe bags, you'll find costume samples, including dresses and shoes. On the CD are some rough drafts for the soundtrack done by a group called The Feelgoods.* After putting on the funky music, Miki poured herself another drink and decided to go inspect the bags of clothing samples.

There were all kinds of outfits she might have worn back in the day, but not even the biggest freak wanted to see her sporting red rhinestone hot pants or a rainbow-hued miniskirt. However, opening the second bag, Miki knew she had found a friend in the wardrobe department when the beautiful maxi-dresses spilled out.

Instantly, an ocean-blue one caught her eye. With sexy slits on the side and a plunging neckline that highlighted her attractive cleavage, the dress fit perfectly. Discarding her mules, she found a pair of gold Versace shoes with pretty straps. Drinking more champagne, a slightly tipsy Miki modeled and danced in front of the mirror.

A few minutes later, there was another knock at her door. Thinking it was the bellhop again, she flung open the door and was shocked to see her costar, Lockhart Williams, standing in the hallway wearing clunky platform shoes, gray double-knit pants, a black mock neck and black leather jacket with the collar and sleeves trimmed in white fur. On his head, he wore a wide-brimmed hat tilted to the side.

"Look at us, both dressed in character like it was Halloween. I'm not sure we should play ourselves in these damn flashback scenes," she smiled.

"Do you think we can get your boy Alex to delete the flashbacks altogether?" Lockhart blurted and busted out laughing. Despite being weary, Miki also cracked up. "I mean, I haven't dressed in these clown clothes since Nixon was in the White House," Lockhart added.

"For some reason, the flashbacks seemed like such a good idea in the script, but you might be right. Unless he shoots us in either smoke or shadows, we're both going to look crazy."

Lockhart looked her up and down and smiled. "Well, at least you look good in your vintage gear. Mine, on the other hand, looks like I'm one of those delusional dudes hanging out in the club, stuck in time and can't let go of the past."

"We might have to change your name to Goldie, like that pimp in *The Mack*," she chuckled as invisible cartoon champagne bubbles floated out of her mouth, drifted toward the ceiling and softly burst. "Can I pour you a drink?"

Opening the door wider, she heard a voice in the back of her head trying to warn her to behave, but she simply ignored it.

"Don't mind if I do, baby girl," he said, slowly stepping into the room. "But first you have to let me step out of these damn platforms." Flopping on the couch, he slipped the shoes off. "Man, I didn't even wear kicks like those when they were in style."

Once the shoes were off, Miki handed him a flute of champagne. Gentlemanly, he bowed his head and raised his glass. "To the most beautiful woman on the production," he said. "Thank you for coming out of retirement, so we could all get jobs. If I had to sign autographs at one more comic book convention, I might've hurt somebody."

The two gulped their drinks and Miki refilled them immediately. As though hearing the music for the first time, Lockhart nodded to the beat. "What you listening to?"

"Some songs Alex sent over, stuff he might use for the soundtrack. Got a bunch of young white guys who play and sing like a bunch of old black guys. These kids today have the best musical technology in the world, but they all want to sound low-fi and dusty like Al Green, Curtis Mayfield or Isaac Hayes."

"Can't say that I blame them," Lockhart joked as he drank the champagne. After they'd listened to a few short musical pieces that were obviously for the theme song and action scenes, the pace slowed down and a haunting Hammond organ blared from the speakers like a midnight train.

Slowly working her way toward the stereo, Miki pressed the repeat button. Assured that the same soulful song would play all night long, she said, "Let's go outside on the terrace." Lockhart held out his hand and Miki grabbed it as though holding on to a life preserver.

Walking through the bedroom, Miki pressed a button and

the glass door slid open. "Now that's style," Williams said. As they gazed toward the clear sky, the quarter moon and the shining stars looked as though one could touch them. "With a view like this, I should get to the fiftieth floor more often."

Sweetly, he held her around the waist as they swayed to the beat. As a haunting saxophone and jazzy guitar gently wept, she was reminded of waterfalls. After the dance, they leaned against the terrace railing and Miki gasped as Lockhart grabbed her ass firmly, pulling her closer.

While she closed her eyes as they made out like horny high school kids, he firmly rubbed his fingers against her sex. Breathing heavy, her scream momentarily drowned out the drums and salsa percussion as the falsetto-singing soul boy on the track moaned lyrics about "autumn rains," "forever" and "don't go away."

Sung in a tone that was sexy and sweet, it made Miki think of warm honey dripping down her belly, sticking to her pubic hair and glazing her clit. "Turn around," Lockhart whispered in her ear; letting go briefly, Miki followed his orders and listened as he unfastened his belt buckle.

Taking a side glance at Lockhart, she saw that he was now completely naked while she was still fully dressed. "Didn't I say turn around?" Lockhart grunted, as he slowly slid the maxi-dress up Miki's tingling body, loving the feel of the silky qiana material on her skin.

Grabbing her by the back of her hair, Lockhart rubbed his cock between her buttcheeks as Miki bent over slightly, anticipating the moment his hardness would enter her. Staring blindly into the lights of the city twinkling in the distance, she squealed and moaned as Lockhart finally blew her mind.

* * *

After shooting the final flashback scene of the day, the hyperactive director stood in front of the cast and showered "returning star Miki Jamison" with compliments about her performance. "I could really feel your hatred for King Johnson," Reid observed. "So much energy and passion."

After Reid invited her to watch the rushes, Miki caught Lockhart's eyes and smiled. Dressed in his character's pimp clothes and platform shoes, he returned her goodwill. Grinning back, Williams shrugged his shoulders and nodded toward the direction leading to their hotel. Having already given him the extra key to her suite, Miki could barely wait to get back to the Sutton.

SPECIAL REQUEST

Rachel Kramer Bussel

I love my job as a hotel concierge, because every day is utterly different from the last. One day I might be called upon to have a treadmill, exercise bike, yoga instructor or Reiki healer sent to a room, another day it might be a pet snake or exotic foodstuff. My hotel specializes in offering anything a customer wants, for a price, and I'm the go-to person, the professional procurer.

I'm paid handsomely for the job—as I should be, considering it involves crazy hours and traversing all the hidden nooks and crannies of Los Angeles, and sometimes other parts of California—but that's not what I love best about it. I love it because I'm a people person, and there's no better job for meeting new people every day than catering to the demands of a high-end hotel's ritziest, most demanding customers. I graduated with a degree in sociology but quickly learned the best way of studying human beings isn't by studying them, but by interacting with them and being privy to their secrets. I was like a special combination of therapist and magician, ready to listen to the oddest of requests and produce the desired results, while sparing my clients any of the tedium of decision-making. All they had to do was decide they wanted something, and I made it happen.

I'd been doing the job for five years, on a lucky break fresh out of college after applying for the job and being sent on what amounted to a scavenger hunt. I received a hefty bonus each year and was treated as a key part of the team. I was at every important meeting, and while my name didn't appear in the hotel's literature or press releases, the fact that we offered every amenity one could imagine was clearly stated. My existence was a little bit under-the-radar, but word got around, and often I'd be requested by name by clients who wouldn't part with the information about their needs unless we were in a locked room and they'd made sure nobody else was listening. Basically, I'm paid to be discreet, discerning, direct and thorough, to listen without judgment. As long as the client can pay our fees, they can have anything flown in from anywhere; they can buy goods, services, and even sex—for the right price. I'd even signed a noncompete, and while I knew I hadn't seen everything, I thought I'd come pretty damn close—but nothing had prepared me for Claudine.

Usually the people making the requests were men. Rich men, sometimes Hollywood stars, since we're located in Beverly Hills; sometimes athletes, sometimes politicians or princes or just your average millionaire or even wild-card billionaire who wants the fluffiest towels, a new designer bathrobe every day, private access to the hot tub, and a pretty woman to fluff the towels, not to mention fluff him if desired. I don't mind even the most obscure requests, since at the end of the day, I know I'm helping brighten someone's visit, and giving them the kind of full service no other hotel can match.

Sometimes it's a couple desiring my services, the husband busy with meetings while the wife wants a guided tour of the best shops and spas, or a partner to hike mountains with. Maybe she'll be dripping with diamonds, and ask for her food to be steamed and spiced to perfection, but with no fat. I'd sought out tattoo artists, feng shui specialists for long-term guests, nutritionists, manicurists, Japanese hair-straightening specialists, and more. But Claudine wanted something entirely different. "This is all confidential, right? You don't have the room bugged or anything, do you?" she asked as I sat in a chair and watched her, my face professional but utterly curious. She was clearly not a lady who lunched—at least, not at any of the high-end see-and-be-seen restaurants my clients usually requested. Her elegance wasn't about designer labels, but an air of both entitlement and sexual power; she radiated her body heat across the room, so I knew it was going to be one of the racier requests I'd handled even before she spoke.

"Of course not. Your privacy and satisfaction are of the utmost importance to us. To me." I was surprised at her cautiousness. She was younger than I'd expected, not a wealthy widow or CEO, but a girl, really, who looked close to my age, twenty-eight. Her clothes were simple enough on the surface, though the jeans were designer, the white blouse clearly silk, the lacy white bra beneath it sturdily sculpted, showcasing her beautiful breasts, and the five-inch leopard-print heels were fierce, proclaiming her a woman not to mess with. There were no flowers in her hair or on her clothing; she was a woman who meant business, even though her business was of a kind only a woman like me could provide.

"So I booked this room because I'd heard from a friend that you will do anything to fulfill your clients' wishes. I've been unable to find anyone who could meet my exact specifications, but you look like you'll know where to find what I need. And my wish is for, well, an orgy. Tomorrow night. I want a room full of hot men and women to pleasure me and each other. Not professionals, just regular sexy people looking to have a good time. And I want you to join us. That's a must. As a guest, off the clock. Confidentially of course—I must make sure not a word of this gets out," Claudine finished with a Cheshire cat–like smile.

I'd just finished telling her I could get her anything she wanted, so I couldn't refuse—not if I wanted to keep my job, not to mention my pride. Instead, I just stared at her, agog. I'd brought in ladies of the night, fetish specialists, pro subs and dominatrices. I'd had people ask me to personally pour them baths full of champagne, and I'd even sipped a little as a recent Oscar winner had extended his gorgeous body into his suite's sumptuous tub while I'd popped cork after cork until he was fully submerged. He'd asked me to join him and while I was very, very tempted, I declined save for the luxury of pouring the chilled bubbly over his shoulders, then splashing the last few drops onto his face and indulging in one of the hottest kisses of my life. I was pretty sure he had a cell phone full of numbers of women who'd be more than willing to slip into his tub, so I'd left him to them.

I did, in fact, have the numbers of plenty of escorts and dominatrices handy, friends who specialized in high-end clients who I trusted implicitly for their discretion and ability to do their job well. But Claudine wanted real people, not professionals—except for, well, me. She wanted people who weren't acting like they wanted to share her bed, but who would be overjoyed to worship her leopard-print heels, not to mention the rest of her. I could tell that she wasn't so much a voyeur or exhibitionist as used to being the centerpiece of any encounter, erotic or otherwise; she'd never be so crass as to say "gang bang" but she wasn't going to be satisfied unless all those hands and mouths were focused on her at some point in the night. I wasn't sure if

I was doing my job or relegating my duties when an image of Claudine with men nibbling on her toes and a woman buried between her legs flashed in my mind.

"Now, if we understand each other, I'm going to slip into a bath. I need to soak my feet." Claudine smiled at me, her glistening red lips curving upward, her brown eyes dancing over my surprised face. She unbuttoned her blouse and dropped it on the bed, then casually reached behind her to unhook her bra, letting her large, clearly natural breasts hang heavily against her, before pausing to finish her instructions.

"I'd love a couple, and maybe some college kids, a girl with some tattoos, a man with a huge cock. A boy I can tie up. With you as my dessert," Claudine added with a laugh before stepping toward me, placing her hand at the back of my head, and giving me a full, passionate kiss, as if that were something she were used to doing with her minions. Her mouth tasted minty and sweet, and her tongue was as possessive as the rest of her. It was the kind of kiss I was used to from men, not women. Her breasts pressed against me, begging me touch them. I was still in shock, but my pussy clearly wasn't, because it responded to her touch, to her tongue darting against mine. She pulled away, then slithered out of her jeans and panties, before waving goodbye and sliding into the bathroom, where the sound of rushing water greeted me. I rubbed at my lips, hoping to remove the lipstick as quickly as I could.

I left and went to my office, opening up my notebook and writing her name at the top. I couldn't believe this. Why would a woman like her come here? I mean, yes, we promised full service, but she was taking that slogan to its grandest possible conclusion, aside from requesting a mountain of coke to roll around in or a chauffeur-driven Lamborghini Aventador. I would've been well within my rights to refuse, or to simply refer her to someone better suited to meeting her needs, yet I didn't want to. It wasn't just the challenge of Claudine's request, or the probable tip, or anything of a professional nature; I *wanted* to be there, as me, Francine, the woman who'd just been kissed by a woman who went after exactly what she desired. I wanted to see, feel, taste, smell and simply luxuriate in being at such a hedonistic event, at my workplace.

This task was naughty yet dutiful, and being either of those was a surefire way to turn me on; combining them was already sending my libido through the roof. I'm not submissive in real life, and barely call myself a sub in the bedroom, but I do like serving, pleasing, providing. It makes me good at my job, and adds a frisson of sexual energy to my day, not to mention making me glad I contributed to the world. No, I'm not off lobbying Congress or anything, but I like to feel that what I put out into the universe is positive, that my existence feeds others, sometimes literally. Plus, there was the mystery factor. I wanted to find out, up close and personal, why Claudine was so eager for this, since she was clearly a woman who could probably walk into any bar, smile, snap her fingers and produce a round of admirers.

I'm not a quitter, but it was more than my work ethic at stake. I liked who Claudine had turned me into in those few minutes alone together, the kind of woman who gets selected and seduced, who other women wanted for real, not just for a quickie make-out session at a bar. I'm mostly into guys, but beautiful women have a seemingly magical effect on me. Plus I'd always wanted to host an orgy myself but had never had the guts to orchestrate that particular fantasy. I'd been to a few, sure, but they'd never quite lived up to my vivid imagination. I had a feeling that even if I invited total losers, Claudine would find a way to spin them into the equivalent of sex-party gold; I was just the conduit.

Alone in my office, I immediately texted my best friend, Tracy, as well as Henry, our mostly gay but into the occasional woman pal, and a couple I knew who made documentaries for money, and documented their own wild swinging sex life for fun. All of them were free Saturday, and Tracy was planning to bring her basketball-player boyfriend, while Henry had a hot young thing he had a date with that night; at the very least, they'd provide some entertainment for the rest of us. He referred me to a queer dyke couple who were more than happy to come once I promised them a free room.

I explained to each of them that this wasn't my idea, but Claudine's, and they were not only sworn to secrecy, but part of the bargain was that they'd have to be amenable to helping Claudine have the best time possible. I didn't want to lose her as a guest, not just for the money, but because I prided myself on retaining our most demanding customers, some of whom had been staying at our hotel for over twenty years, since long before my tenure.

I went to bed that night and deliberately didn't masturbate, wanting to save myself for the following night. I woke up early from a feverish dream in which Claudine had wrapped a slim silver chain around my neck and was leading me around by it, taking me on a tour of the hallways I walked purposefully in my heels every day, while I simultaneously reveled in being potentially seen by customers and blushed at the thought.

I was in full party-planning mode, and each action only made me wetter. I bought lube and gloves and condoms; nipple clamps, dildos, butt plugs. I filled a whole basket at the sex-toy store, causing even the jaded clerk to raise his eyebrows at the large bill, and my use of a corporate card to pay for it. Normally, I have little patience with nosy clerks, but this time I sized him up and decided on the spot to offer him an invitation. "I'm hosting a party. Well, my new friend is. It's at this address, in this room. You're invited, if you think you can handle it, Patrick," I said as I signed the bill. He looked a little stunned, but he smiled and stammered and said he'd try to make it.

I bought a selection of snacks and sodas and alcohol, programmed my iPod and made sure the rooms on either side of Claudine's were free. One of them opened up to a suite, and as for the other, I didn't want to risk someone booking it and them being subjected to what surely wouldn't be a quiet crowd. Then it was my turn to get ready. What does a girl wear to an orgy? I sifted through my outfits, then my lingerie drawer, finally concluding that what I wore, aside from a smile, didn't really matter. It was more about bringing the real me, the woman who wasn't a type-A perfectionist but was a woman, one who wanted to please and be pleased, to make herself happy by hearing Claudine moan. And, yes, I wanted to see Claudine crack a little, wanted to see the cool veneer of rich-lady power crumble into a screaming orgasm, or five.

So I simply wore a lacy black slip over a lacy hot-pink slip, with a plain black coat that covered each. My five-inch heels accentuated my calves, including the string of pearls tattooed onto the right one. The half-open oyster shell near my hip was hidden, but would soon be revealed. "Calm down, everything's going to be fine," I said out loud, a mantra I'd taken to repeating when my world seemed to be collapsing.

I put everything I needed into my trunk, drove to valet parking, and told Marc to bring everything to Claudine's room in a few minutes. Then I spoke with Gerald, the manager on duty, presenting him with a firm guest list. "No one else, including staff, is to come up to her room unless you clear it with me first. Got it?" He looked at me searchingly but didn't ask questions. That's what I liked about Gerald; it would've made him a poor detective, but he was a valuable employee to have on your side.

When I knocked on her door, I got a sudden chill. I knew Claudine would like the motley crew I'd selected for our evening's entertainment; how could she not? But what about me? Would I be a bit player or her costar? And which did I prefer? Claudine peeked around the edge of the door. "Come in, my sweet," she said, and shut the door right after me. She was completely naked, and up close, I could see she had at least a dozen years on my twenty-seven, and in all likelihood was in her late forties, but her body was beautiful nonetheless. I was impressed that, unlike me, she hadn't tried to adorn herself; her naked body simply said, "Here I am, ready for the taking."

"Let me get a good look at you," she said, whisking off my coat when my fingers fumbled with the buttons, then instructing me to twirl around, then lift the hem of my slips. I'd no sooner bared my thong-adorned ass than there was a knock on the door. I reached for the coat, but Claudine ordered me to sit on the bed. She opened the door the same way she had with me and Marc entered, pushing a luggage cart and almost dropping the bag in his hand when he saw me nude. I winked at him, and he continued unloading everything, earning him a tip that Claudine made sure to stuff down his pants. Once the door had closed behind him, she said, "Now, where were we? Oh yes, you were showing me your outfit." Her laugh filled the room. "Show me again."

Claudine stepped closer and I searched her eyes, wanting to please her. I was doing something bold, but inside I felt shy as I pulled up the slips to reveal the outline of my pussy lips, spared from view only by a small strip of fabric. "Take those off," Claudine said, her voice huskier, and under her watchful eye, I slithered out of the thong, letting it land on the carpet. Claudine shuddered, then reached for the nightstand. As she moved toward me, I saw she had a silk blindfold heading for my face. Letting her put it on would be the ultimate test: could I be in control of my job, of the party I'd organized, while submitting to someone else's control? The questions must've been written on my face, because Claudine said, "Yes. Yes. Give yourself to me, Francine."

I decided this was a case of something being worth doing only if you went all the way with it. Besides, I wasn't really in charge at all; Claudine could kick out all my guests if she wanted to. She could report me for some made-up transgression. She'd been in control since that first kiss. I was immediately rewarded, because once the blindfold was on, the white noise in my head dissipated, as if by not being able to see, I couldn't hear all the worries and fears that usually clamored for space in my psyche. Instead, all I heard and felt were Claudine's movements. She positioned me so my head was back against the pillows, my arms above my head. Soon she was fastening cuffs around my wrists. "How does that feel?" she asked. I tugged and smiled, because I liked that too. I was submitting, surrendering, and getting wetter by the second.

"You probably thought I wanted to be the star of the party," she said, once again uncannily reading my mind. "I'm much more of a voyeur, my dear, though I do plan to participate. But if anyone's the star, it's going to be you. I want to watch the pretty boys and girls having their way with you, touching you, taking you, filling you. I want to make sure you thoroughly enjoy this hotel room that I'm paying for. You deserve it. And so do I." I didn't ask why that might be the case, because I soon heard a buzzing sound, followed by the press of a vibrator against my clit. I dropped my knees wider and was so lost in the sensations of being bound and being buzzed that I barely heard the door. Claudine wrapped my hand around the vibrator and left to answer it. Voices soon filled the room, and part of me wished I could greet people in a less exposed way. But Claudine was smart: being blindfolded meant I couldn't see the reactions the others were having to me, couldn't assess whether my outfit, my body, measured up to theirs.

"Sweetie!" Tracy said, rushing over to kiss me on the cheek and grant me a dusting of perfume and powder. "You look like you're enjoying yourself." I was, and I kept on enjoying myself, until someone took the toy from my hand, and someone else started sucking on one nipple. I knew I'd only invited nine people, but it felt like I was in the center of dozens of hungry men and women. "She's gorgeous, isn't she?" I heard Claudine pronounce, as if displaying a piece of very modern art she'd sculpted herself. Perhaps she had, because this version of me, the one sprawled naked across a bed in my place of work getting filled and fondled and kissed and sucked, wasn't someone I'd ever have produced on my own.

I turned toward her voice and smiled, suddenly hungry for her. She'd turned the tables on me thoroughly, tricking me into thinking she wanted to be the star, when really she wanted to be the director of her own personal sex show.

I could hear Tracy murmuring near me, then gasping, as Alex, her boyfriend, did something exquisite to her. "Can I have a turn?" Claudine's voice said near me. I wanted to see what she was going to get her turn doing, but just then my legs were spread even wider and something big and slippery with lube was pressed against my center. At first, I strained to listen and to decipher what exactly was going on, but I figured out fast that if I relaxed, the toy would not only enter me farther and faster, but I could fully immerse myself in the many sounds and sensations going on around me.

"I think Francine deserves a raise, don't you?" I heard Claudine asking someone even as the sounds of hard spankings rang through the air.

"Yes," Tracy let out, and then I heard more than one hand slapping skin, and remembered Tracy telling me that Alex sometimes liked to strike her across the face, and she'd quickly grown to love it. Tears rushed to my covered eyes, tears of pleasure, especially when someone rushed in and used nipple clamps—likely a pair that I'd purchased—and fastened them on my buds.

There was a knock at the door. "Whoever could that be? Well, Francine invited everyone, so she should answer," Claudine said, and shifted her body to lick along my neck. The toy eased out of me, but the blindfold and clamps stayed on.

I walked to the door and called out, as casually as I could, "Who is it?"

"Patrick. From the store."

Damn. Well, I couldn't turn him away, so I opened the door as carefully as I could and said, "Hurry."

I wished I could see his face, to see if he was grinning at me, but I couldn't. He handed something to me. "Thank you," I said automatically, then paused. How to explain my outfit—or rather, lack of one?

"Welcome," called out Claudine. "Please feel free to set those chocolates out, I'm sure they will be greatly appreciated, as are you, pretty boy." I blushed, and smiled at where I thought Patrick was standing. "Francine, come back here," she called to me, and I did. "Do join in. An orgy's not truly an orgy unless everyone's participating, don't you think?"

"Sure," he said, sounding slightly uncertain, which endeared him to me. If I was in over my head, I had no choice but to keep going. You can't exactly kick everyone out when it's not really your party. Besides, it was fun, when I let myself enjoy it. Then Patrick pulled me close. I knew it was him because he told me. "You look beautiful, even better than you did at the store, and that's saying something." His breath was sweet, minty, his mouth warm. He kissed me like we were alone, his tongue slowly slithering into my mouth. He climbed on top of me, and I figured the other orgy-goers were occupying themselves because nobody seemed to bother with us. "Is this okay?" Patrick asked as he started to take off his pants.

"Yes," I said. "I want to feel you." I almost added, "I don't normally do this," which, while true, was unnecessary. There's no room for modesty at an orgy. Our private moment was interrupted by Claudine whispering in my ear. "Are you enjoying yourself? I am," she said, then kissed all along my earlobe, my neck, my cheek, then my lips. She fed me each breast, her necklace dangling in my face as Patrick entered me. I was more than ready, having been primed by the dildo. I could tell he was wearing a condom, and I could also tell he was big, wonderfully so.

"I am enjoying myself," I said as she kissed me for a long time, before shifting so I could lick her pussy. Claudine rubbed herself against my tongue, and the more she did, the more I liked it. The room was filled with the sounds of sex, and spanking, and kissing. The noises swirled around me as I ate Claudine, then shifted so that both Patrick and I could pleasure Claudine.

Only after we'd exhausted every possible position was I allowed to take off the blindfold. The familiar room looked different, and not just because there were so many naked bodies strewn across it. Then I looked down at myself, at the lipstick smeared on my body, the metal clamps tight on my nubs, my lingerie on the floor. I was the one who was different. I'd procured, and been procured. I'd more than met Claudine's demands, and in return she'd tipped my world on its side. I knew that from that moment on, I was never going to look at my hotel in the same way again.

ABOUT THE AUTHORS

VALERIE ALEXANDER is a writer who lives in Arizona. Her work has been previously published in *Best Lesbian Erotica, Best of Best Women's Erotica, Gotta Have It* and other anthologies.

TENILLE BROWN is a Southern, shoe-shopping, wine-drinking writer whose erotica has been published online and in over thirty print anthologies including *Ultimate Lesbian Erotica 2007, Fast Girls, Making the Hook Up, Iridescence, F Is for Fetish* and *Best Bondage Erotica 2011*. She blogs at thesteppingstone.blogspot.com and tweets @TheRealTenille.

LILY K. CHO is a bisexual, married mom living in the San Francisco Bay Area. Lily has collected erotica for twenty-five years, is a member of Mensa and thinks we should celebrate our unique qualities! Her work has been selected for the erotic anthology *One Night Only*. Write her at lilykcho@gmail.com.

With coauthors and on her own, **ANDREA DALE** (cyvarwydd.com) has sold two novels to Virgin Books UK and approximately one hundred stories to Harlequin Spice, Avon Red and Cleis Press, among others. She confesses that this story was blatantly inspired by Rick Springfield's "Jessie's Girl."

DELILAH DEVLIN is an author with a rapidly expanding reputation for writing deliciously edgy stories with complex characters. Whether creating dark, erotically charged paranormal worlds or richly descriptive westerns that ring with authenticity, Delilah Devlin "pens in uncharted territory that will leave the readers breathless and hungering for more..." (Paranormal Romance Reviews).

JUSTINE ELYOT is an author of erotica and erotic romance for a range of publishers including Black Lace, Xcite Books, Carina Press, Cleis Press and Total E-Bound. She likes light erotica and dark romance, and vice versa.

EROBINTICA is the sex-obsessed persona of writer and poet Robin Elizabeth Sampson. She's been included in *Coming Together: Al Fresco* and in *Eat Me: Seven Stories of Gluttony*. Her poetry made the 2010 Seattle Erotic Art Festival and she's read at Philadelphia's Erotic Literary Salon. Her blog is erobintica.blogspot.com.

SUZANNE FOX lives and works in Cornwall, England, where she loves to relax in the beautiful and inspiring outdoors. Suzanne has enjoyed taking part in many murder weekends and particularly enjoys it when the lines between fantasy and reality become blurred.

ABOUT THE AUTHORS

Film junkie and erotica writer **MICHAEL A. GONZALES** has written about pop culture for *Wax Poetics, Stop Smiling, New York* and the *London Telegraph*. His sex writing has appeared in *Brown Sugar 2, Gotta Have It: 69 Stories of Sudden Sex* and *Best Sex Writing 2005*. He lives in Brooklyn.

ARIEL GRAHAM lives with her husband in Northern Nevada. A full-time writer, her work has appeared in multiple anthologies including *Please, Sir* and *Please, Ma'am*, as well as websites such as Torquere and Pink Flamingo. When not writing or procrastinating about writing, she's often running or creating disasters in the kitchen. She tends to keep cats.

TAHIRA IQBAL (tahiraiqbal.com) is a UK-based writer who thoroughly enjoyed her research into the world of five-star hotels and the sexy decadence they offer. You can check out her erotic vampire short story "The Queen" in the *Red Velvet and Absinthe* anthology published by Cleis Press.

STEVE ISAAK, sometimes published under the nom de plume Nikki Isaak, is the author of two anthologies, *Can't sleep: poems, 1987–2007* and *Charge of the scarlet b-sides: microsex stories & poems* (available at Lulu.com). He is also a contributor and editor of two sites, readingbypublight.blogspot.com and the multiauthor microstoryaweek.blogspot.com.

ANNA MEADOWS is a part-time executive assistant, part-time lesbian housewife. Her work appears in six Cleis Press anthologies, including *Steamlust: Steampunk Erotic Romance* and *Girls Who Bite: Lesbian Vampire Erotica*. She lives and writes in Northern California.

EMILY MORETON has been writing since childhood, and now writes mostly contemporary gay erotic short stories, which have appeared in anthologies with a variety of publishers, including two for charity. She lives in Bristol, UK, where she works in the violence against women and girls field.

REMITTANCE GIRL lives and works in Vietnam, where she grows orchids and nurses a sick mango tree.

ELIZABETH SILVER is an erotic romance author, a self-proclaimed Internet junkie and an international woman of mystery. She can be found writing in diners, libraries and coffee shops, either working on fiction or blogging polyamorously at various places, including her website at UrbanSilver.net.

An editor by trade and a romance reader by choice, **SULEIKHA SNYDER** has always dreamed of being a published author. These days, she's finally focusing on making those dreams come true. Suleikha lives in relative obscurity, but you can find her on Twitter at twitter.com/suleikhasnyder.

DONNA GEORGE STOREY is the author of *Amorous Woman*, a steamy novel about an American woman's love affair with Japan. Her short fiction has appeared in numerous journals and anthologies including *Passion: Erotic Romance for Women*, *Penthouse* and *Best Women's Erotica*. Read more of her work at DonnaGeorgeStorey.com.

ELLIE VOKES is a human development major at the University of Maine. She writes in her spare time. She is an avid reader, both of erotica and general fiction.

ABOUT THE EDITOR

RACHEL KRAMER BUSSEL (rachelkramerbussel.com) is a New York–based author, editor and blogger. She has edited over forty books of erotica, including *Women in Lust, Irresistible, Obsessed, Gotta Have It; Best Bondage Erotica 2011 and 2012; Her Surrender; Obsessed; Orgasmic; Bottoms Up: Spanking Good Stories; Spanked; Naughty Spanking Stories from A to Z 1* and *2; Fast Girls; Smooth; Passion; The Mile High Club; Do Not Disturb; Tasting Him; Tasting Her; Please, Sir; Please, Ma'am; He's on Top; She's on Top; Caught Looking; Hide and Seek; Crossdressing; Irresistible* and *Rubber Sex*. She is the *Best Sex Writing* series editor, and winner of six IPPY (Independent Publisher) Awards. Her work has been published in over one hundred anthologies, including *Best American Erotica 2004* and *2006;* Zane's *Chocolate Flava 2* and *Purple Panties; Everything You Know About Sex Is Wrong; Single State of the Union* and *Desire: Women Write About Wanting*. Most recently, she served as senior editor at *Penthouse Vari-*

ation, and wrote the popular "Lusty Lady" column for *The Village Voice.*

Rachel is a sex columnist for SexisMagazine.com and has written for *AVN, Bust,* Cleansheets.com, *Cosmopolitan, Curve,* The Daily Beast, Fresh Yarn, TheFrisky.com, Gothamist, Huffington Post, *Inked,* Mediabistro, *Newsday, New York Post, Penthouse, Playgirl, Radar,* Salon, *San Francisco Chronicle, Time Out New York* and *Zink,* among others. She has appeared on "The Martha Stewart Show," "The Berman and Berman Show," NY1 and Showtime's "Family Business." She hosted the popular In the Flesh Erotic Reading Series (inthefleshreadingseries.com), featuring readers from Susie Bright to Zane, and speaks at conferences, does readings and teaches erotic writing workshops across the country. She blogs at lustylady.blogspot.com.

More from Rachel Kramer Bussel

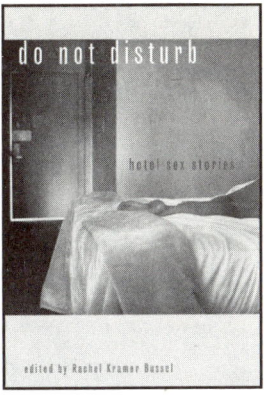

Buy 4 books, Get 1 FREE*

Do Not Disturb
Hotel Sex Stories
Edited by Rachel Kramer Bussel

A delicious array of hotel hookups where it seems like anything can happen—and quite often does. "If *Do Not Disturb* were a hotel, it would a 5-star hotel with the luxury of 24/7 entertainment available."—Erotica Revealed
978-1-57344-344-9 $14.95

Bottoms Up
Spanking Good Stories
Edited by Rachel Kramer Bussel

As sweet as it is kinky, *Bottoms Up* will propel you to pick up a paddle and share in both pleasure and pain, or perhaps simply turn the other cheek.
ISBN 978-1-57344-362-3 $14.95

Orgasmic
Erotica for Women
Edited by Rachel Kramer Bussel

What gets you off? Let *Orgasmic* count the ways...with 25 stories focused on female orgasm, there is something here for every reader.
ISBN 978-1-57344-402-6 $14.95

Please, Sir
Erotic Stories of Female Submission
Edited by Rachel Kramer Bussel

These 22 kinky stories celebrate the thrill of submission by women who know exactly what they want.
ISBN 978-1-57344-389-0 $14.95

Fast Girls
Erotica for Women
Edited by Rachel Kramer Bussel

Fast Girls celebrates the girl with a reputation, the girl who goes all the way, and the girl who doesn't know how to say "no."
ISBN 978-1-57344-384-5 $14.95

* Free book of equal or lesser value. Shipping and applicable sales tax extra.
Cleis Press • (800) 780-2279 • orders@cleispress.com
www.cleispress.com

Red Hot Erotic Romance

Buy 4 books, Get 1 FREE*

Obsessed
Erotic Romance for Women
Edited by Rachel Kramer Bussel

These stories sizzle with the kind of obsession that is fueled by our deepest desires, the ones that hold couples together, the ones that haunt us and don't let go. Whether just-blooming passions, rekindled sparks or reinvented relationships, these lovers put the object of their obsession first.
ISBN 978-1-57344-718-8 $14.95

Passion
Erotic Romance for Women
Edited by Rachel Kramer Bussel

Love and sex have always been intimately intertwined—and *Passion* shows just how delicious the possibilities are when they mingle in this sensual collection edited by award-winning author Rachel Kramer Bussel.
ISBN 978-1-57344-415-6 $14.95

Girls Who Bite
Lesbian Vampire Erotica
Edited by Delilah Devlin

Bestselling romance writer Delilah Devlin and her contributors add fresh girl-on-girl blood to the pantheon of the paranormal. The stories in *Girls Who Bite* are varied, unexpected, and soul-scorching.
ISBN 978-1-57344-715-7 $14.95

Irresistible
Erotic Romance for Couples
Edited by Rachel Kramer Bussel

This prolific editor has gathered the most popular fantasies and created a sizzling, no-holds-barred collection of explicit encounters in which couples turn their deepest desires into reality.
978-1-57344-762-1 $14.95

Heat Wave
Hot, Hot, Hot Erotica
Edited by Alison Tyler

What could be sexier or more seductive than bare, sun-warmed skin? Bestselling erotica author Alison Tyler gathers explicit stories of summer sex bursting with the sweet eroticism of swimsuits, sprinklers, and ripe strawberries.
ISBN 978-1-57344-710-2 $15.95

* Free book of equal or lesser value. Shipping and applicable sales tax extra.
Cleis Press • (800) 780-2279 • orders@cleispress.com
www.cleispress.com

Bestselling Erotica for Couples

Buy 4 books, Get 1 FREE*

Sweet Life
Erotic Fantasies for Couples
Edited by Violet Blue

Your ticket to a front row seat for first-time spankings, breathtaking role-playing scenes, sex parties, women who strap it on and men who love to take it, not to mention threesomes of every combination.
ISBN 978-1-57344-133-9 $14.95

Sweet Life 2
Erotic Fantasies for Couples
Edited by Violet Blue

"This is a we-did-it-you-can-too anthology of real couples playing out their fantasies." —Lou Paget, author of *365 Days of Sensational Sex*
ISBN 978-1-57344-167-4 $15.95

Sweet Love
Erotic Fantasies for Couples
Edited by Violet Blue

"If you ever get a chance to try out your number-one fantasies in real life—and I assure you, there will be more than one—say yes. It's well worth it. May this book, its adventurous authors, and the daring and satisfied characters be your guiding inspiration."—Violet Blue
ISBN 978-1-57344-381-4 $14.95

Afternoon Delight
Erotica for Couples
Edited by Alison Tyler

"Alison Tyler evokes a world of heady sensuality where fantasies are fearlessly explored and dreams gloriously realized."
—Barbara Pizio, Executive Editor, *Penthouse Variations*
ISBN 978-1-57344-341-8 $14.95

Three-Way
Erotic Stories
Edited by Alison Tyler

"Three means more of everything. Maybe I'm greedy, but when it comes to sex, I like more. More fingers. More tongues. More limbs. More tangling and wrestling on the mattress."
ISBN 978-1-57344-193-3 $15.95

---

* Free book of equal or lesser value. Shipping and applicable sales tax extra.
Cleis Press • (800) 780-2279 • orders@cleispress.com
www.cleispress.com

Ordering is easy! Call us toll free or fax us to place your MC/VISA order. You can also mail the order form below with payment to: Cleis Press, 2246 Sixth St., Berkeley, CA 94710.

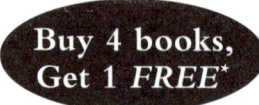

Buy 4 books, Get 1 *FREE**

ORDER FORM

QTY	TITLE	PRICE
_____	_____	_____
_____	_____	_____
_____	_____	_____
_____	_____	_____
_____	_____	_____
_____	_____	_____
_____	_____	_____
	SUBTOTAL	_____
	SHIPPING	_____
	SALES TAX	_____
	TOTAL	_____

Add $3.95 postage/handling for the first book ordered and $1.00 for each additional book. Outside North America, please contact us for shipping rates. California residents add 8.75% sales tax. Payment in U.S. dollars only.

* Free book of equal or lesser value. Shipping and applicable sales tax extra.

Cleis Press • Phone: (800) 780-2279 • Fax: (510) 845-8001
orders@cleispress.com • www.cleispress.com
You'll find more great books on our website

Follow us on Twitter @cleispress • Friend/fan us on Facebook